See No EVIL

ANNE SCHRAFF

SADDLEBACK
EDUCATIONAL PUBLISHING

URBAN UNDERGROUND ®

SADDLEBACK
EDUCATIONAL PUBLISHING
www.sdlback.com

© 2012 by Saddleback Educational Publishing

ISBN-13: 978-1-61651-663-5
ISBN-10: 1-61651-663-1
eBook: 978-1-61247-357-4

Printed in Guangzhou, China
1011/CA21101701

17 16 15 14 13   1 2 3 4 5

CHAPTER ONE

Jaris Spain's parents were talking in the living room about their fourteen-year-old daughter, Chelsea. Last year, she had been in eighth grade at Marian Anderson Middle School. At that time, she and two friends did a very foolish and dangerous thing. They accepted a ride from two guys in a Mercedes. One of the guys was a student at Tubman High School. They knew him, and the other guy was his brother. Chelsea, Athena Edson, and Keisha all climbed into the Mercedes for a ride around the block. The ride turned out to be a lot longer, sometimes at speeds of over one hundred miles an hour. Chelsea's parents were terrified

1

and angry. Chelsea had been biking, walking, and taking the bus wherever she needed to go. Now she was grounded. Now the job of taking her to and from school fell to her seventeen-year-old brother, Jaris. Now Chelsea had become a freshman at Harriet Tubman High School. She was earning good grades, and she had accepted her punishment with grace.

Lorenzo and Monica Spain were the parents of Jaris and Chelsea. And they were now considering lifting the restriction on Chelsea. They thought her responsible behavior had earned her her freedom. Chelsea was nearing her fifteenth birthday, and maybe it was time for her to be on her own again. Chelsea was spending time at Athena Edson's house along with another friend, Inessa Weaver.

"What do you think, Lorenzo?" Mom asked. "Chelsea has been doing really well in school, and she could ride her bike or even walk to Tubman with Inessa. There aren't any dangerous intersections between here and there. Maybe it's time we give her more responsibility."

Pop wasn't so sure. "The little girl has been doing better, yeah," he granted. "But she still hangs with that loose cannon, Athena. Who knows what the two of them might dream up? Then those little punks sniffin' around. Maurice Moore, I can't stand him. Swaggering little pup. Heston Crawford is some better. I don't mind him so much. I don't know, Monie."

"Well, why don't we just try it?" Mom suggested. "Let Chelsea go to school on her own for a couple weeks, and see how it goes. Lorenzo, she hasn't complained or anything, but I know she feels real stifled. I mean, most of the freshman kids who live this close to Tubman get there on their own. I hate to have her start thinking that we don't trust her at all—and *never will*."

"Yeah," Pop relented slowly. "You got a point there. It's like the old sayin', 'If I got the name, I might as well have the game.'"

"Exactly," Mom responded, relieved that her husband was coming around. Lorenzo Spain was a very stubborn man, but Monica knew that no father loved his children more. Many other fathers were occasionally involved, but Lorenzo was a dad twenty-four-seven.

"You be the one who tells her, Lorenzo," Mom suggested. "She adores you. And it's really been hard on her knowing how she let you down so bad when she went riding with those dopeheads. When you go over to Athena's house to pick her up tonight, you tell her that tomorrow she can go to Tubman on her own."

"Okay, Monie," Pop agreed. He saw his tall son, Jaris, now a senior at Tubman, standing nearby and listening. "What do you think of what we decided, Jaris? We doing the right thing?" Pop asked. "You know the little girl maybe better than we do. Is she ready for prime time?"

"Yeah, I think so," Jaris replied. He wasn't saying that only because he was tired of driving Chelsea to and from school and the mall. He really noticed that Chelsea was getting more mature. He didn't think she'd be accepting rides from dopeheads anymore.

Jaris truly felt that Chelsea was ready for more freedom and that she wouldn't abuse it. She had to learn sometime to be responsible without someone standing at her side.

Pop climbed into his pickup truck at nine o'clock and made the short drive over to Athena Edson's house. He didn't like the Edsons. They gave Athena way too much freedom, he thought. They were both so wrapped up in their own jobs, they paid little attention to their daughter. Pop would have preferred Chelsea not being friends with Athena, but the girls were inseparable. Pop feared that Athena appealed to Chelsea's wild side, and that thought worried him.

When Pop rang the doorbell at the Edson house, he expected one of the parents to answer. Instead, Athena opened the door. "Hi, Mr. Spain," she said, swinging the door open. She was a beautiful girl. Too beautiful, Pop thought. She wore sparkly tight tops and skinny jeans. She looked more like a sixteen- or seventeen-year-old than what she was—a fourteen-year-old just out of middle school.

"Hi there, Athena," Pop responded. "So who's home, Mom or Dad?"

"Mom had to go to a faculty meeting at her high school, and Pop is seeing a client or something, I don't know," Athena answered lightheartedly.

"Beautiful!" Pop commented. Pop walked into the living room, where Chelsea and Inessa were downloading music. "Three little girls home all by themselves. Lissen up girls, just now I ring the doorbell. Right away Athena here, she flings open the door. Don't even look through the peephole. No. Just flings open the door. I mighta been Jack the Ripper, and now here I am in the living room with you guys."

Chelsea giggled. "Who's Jack the Ripper, Pop?" she asked.

"He wasn't a nice man," Pop explained. "And don't make a joke of it. It ain't funny, little girl. Athena, don't be doin' airhead stunts like that. You just don't open the door before you look through the peephole and see who it is, okay? Some bad people out there in the dark. You don't just open the door and invite them in whoever they are."

"You're right, Mr. Spain," Inessa agreed grimly. She was the most sensible of the trio. "I've told Athena the same thing. And for your information, Chelsea, Jack the Ripper was a horrible murderer who lived in London, England. He murdered a lot of girls."

Chelsea stopped smiling. "I'm sorry, Pop," she apologized.

Pop was fuming, already having second thoughts about lifting Chelsea's restrictions. "I let you come over here," he declared "and in two seconds of me being

here, I see stuff that's wrong and dangerous. Athena, stop with the music, okay?
Who's pickin' you up, Inessa?"

"My mom will be here pretty soon,"
Inessa replied.

"Okay then, come on Chelsea, we're
goin' home," Pop commanded. Chelsea
jumped up and joined her father. She might
have been fourteen going on fifteen, but to
Lorenzo Spain she was about eleven years
old. She was his little girl who was jumping
rope only yesterday and who still had all
her stuffed animals arranged on her bed.

After Chelsea was in the truck, Pop
commented, "You ain't been riding your
bike too much lately, little girl."

"No," Chelsea answered sadly, "I can't
go anywhere, you know."

"Would you like to be riding your bike
again, little girl?" Pop asked.

"Oh Pop!" Chelsea screamed, clasping
her cheeks with her hands.

"Maybe you could bike to school again,
you think?" Pop continued.

CHAPTER ONE

Chelsea leaned over and gave her father a big kiss on the cheek. "Oh Pop," she cried, "you mean—"

"Your mom and I, we were talkin'," Pop went on. "You been doin' real good in school, Chelsea. You're gettin' good grades. Teachers all sayin' good stuff about you. You been mindin' your Ps and Qs, if you know what I mean. So you think you can handle bikin' or walkin' to school again when the weather is nice? When it's rainin' we'll get you there."

"Ohhh!" Chelsea cried, "That would be so wonderful. I love to ride my bike to school or walk with Inessa. Most of the time we walk, and it's so fun to talk to my friends. Oh Pop, I can text my friends on the way to school and—"

"Remember now," Pop insisted sternly, "no talkin' on the phone or texting anybody while you're on your bike. You gotta be watchin' the road."

"Yeah, right, Pop," Chelsea agreed. "You mean I can start tomorrow?"

"I guess so," Pop said.

Chelsea grabbed her cell phone. Within seconds, she had Inessa on the line. "Inessa! You'll never guess," she cried. "We can ride our bikes to school tomorrow. I'm not kidding! I got out of jail. I'm on parole now!"

As he walked into the house, Pop made the announcement. "We got it settled, babe. Chelsea's riding to school on her bike tomorrow. She's walkin' on air."

Mom smiled, and Chelsea flew into her arms, hugging her. "Thanks, Mom. Oh, goin' to school will be so fun now!"

"You know what, though, Monie," Pop added, getting serious. "No more sleep-overs at Athena's house. Her idiot parents leave those kids alone while they go traipsing around to their various places. I hit the doorbell, and that airhead Athena, she don't even check who I am. She just flings open the door."

Pop turned to his daughter. "Chelsea, lissen up," he commanded. "Any sleepovers gonna be over here or at Inessa's or Keisha's house. That Trudy Edson, the big shot high school teacher, she don't know how to parent. And her husband is no good either. Kids shouldn't be left alone like that. There's Athena just opening up to anybody."

"You're right, Lorenzo," Mom agreed. "Did you hear that, Chelsea? No more sleepovers at Athena's house."

"Uh-huh," Chelsea said, hurrying to her room to text all her friends with the good news. She wasn't grounded anymore. She was free! As Chelsea ran down the hall, she almost collided with Jaris. "Did you hear?" she cried.

"Yeah, chili pepper, way to go," Jaris said.

Chelsea could scarcely sleep thinking about the next morning. At breakfast, she wolfed down her eggs and bacon and gulped her orange juice.

"Inessa is out there already," Jaris noted.

"Chelsea," Mom scolded, "you've got to eat your breakfast like a normal person. I know you're excited about biking to school, but you'll get indigestion!"

Chelsea grabbed her backpack and raced out the door. "Bye Mom! Bye Pop! Bye Jare!" she screamed over her shoulder.

"Hi, Chelsea," Inessa said when she saw her. "I didn't really believe you were getting to ride your bike to school again."

The two girls climbed on their bikes and headed for Tubman High School.

"You can see the ghoul house this morning," Inessa remarked. She had been telling Chelsea about an old house that was foreclosed on months ago on Navaho Street. Sometimes strange sounds came out of it. It seemed like someone was screaming, and at other times there were shrieks. The bank had put up a sign warning against trespassing.

"I bet people live in there," Inessa guessed. "Maybe homeless people. It was on TV that people who got nowhere to stay sometimes camp in the foreclosed houses."

"Did you ever go look in the windows?" Chelsea asked.

"No way!" Inessa cried. "Athena said she did once. Athena's such an idiot, she's not afraid or anything. It was at night, and she was with Maurice Moore. They were just hanging around the twenty-four-seven store. On their way home, they looked in the windows of the ghoul house. Athena swears she saw people walking around, but I think she was lying. Sometimes I think Athena is crazy."

"Did Maurice see anything?" Chelsea asked, as they pedaled along.

"He said he didn't see anything," Inessa answered. "But Athena said she saw a few skinny gray people."

"Is that the house?" Chelsea asked, spotting a broken-down house with a fore-closure sign out front.

"Yeah," Inessa said.

"We're early, Inessa," Chelsea noted. "Let's just take a quick peek."

"I don't want to," Inessa replied. "It says no trespassing. Come on, Chelsea. Do you want to get in trouble the very first day you're off restrictions?"

Chelsea slowed her bike and stopped. "Just a quick peek," she said, leaning her bike against a brick wall.

Inessa sat on her bike, glaring at Chelsea. "I'm not looking in that window, Chelsea Spain, and you shouldn't be doing it either!"

"Aw, it's no big deal," Chelsea chided. She walked through the tall dead grass to the window. The door had been boarded up by the bank. But somebody had torn part of the plywood away, and she could look in. There was a lot of dust on the window, and spiderwebs crisscrossed it.

"It looks real spooky," Chelsea called back to Inessa.

"Come on, Chelsea, let's go. We'll be late for school!" Inessa yelled.

Chelsea thought that sometimes Inessa could be such a wet blanket. "The room looks all messy. There's an old chair and—" Suddenly they both heard a long drawn-out scream, like you hear in horror movies. Chelsea almost fell down racing from the window back to her bike. "Oh Inessa, did you hear *that*?" she cried. Her legs were numb. She wanted to pedal away faster, but she could barely get her legs to work. Gradually, the girls put distance between them and the house.

"*I told you not to go near the ghoul house!*" Inessa scolded. "I told you, but you never listen! You better watch yourself, Chelsea Spain. You'll get in trouble again, and you'll be grounded all over again!"

"But what *was* that?" Chelsea stammered.

"It's been going on for a good long time," Inessa commented. "When I ride my bike on Navaho Street, I hear it."

"Did you tell your parents, Inessa?" Chelsea asked.

"No," Inessa responded. "If I told them about the ghoul house, maybe they wouldn't let me ride my bike to school either. And don't you go telling anybody either, Chelsea. You know how your pop is. He'll make a big deal out of it."

"But what if somebody is hurt or something and needs help?" Chelsea asked.

"Come on, girl, don't be stupid. It's been going on like that for more than a month. The neighbors must hear it," Inessa said.

"Maybe the bank rigged something up to scare people from going in and stealing stuff," Chelsea suggested.

Maurice Moore and Heston Crawford were jogging to school and caught up with them. The girls stopped their bikes.

"Hey, Chelsea," Maurice yelled. "You're riding your bike again. Cool!"

"Yeah, I'm not grounded anymore," Chelsea explained. She had texted Heston about being off restrictions, but she wasn't close enough to Maurice to text him.

"That's a hot little top you got on there, girl," Maurice noted with a grin.

"Thanks," Chelsea responded. "Hey Maurice, what about that ghoul house? What do you think is going on there?"

"It's haunted," Maurice stated, matter-of-factly.

"Don't be ridiculous, Maurice," Inessa said. "There's no such thing as a haunted house."

"I looked in with Athena one night. I didn't see them, but Athena did," Maurice claimed.

"See who?" Chelsea demanded.

"The ghosts," Maurice answered. "They were skinny and gray, and they looked like they were made out of smoke. That's what Athena said."

Heston Crawford laughed. "That's stupid. Inessa's right. There's no such thing as ghosts."

"How do you know, Heston?" Maurice asked. "Lotta stuff going on that we don't know about."

Maurice walked alongside Chelsea's bike, and he spoke softly to her. "I ain't forgot."

"Forgot what?" Chelsea asked him.

"Remember when we just started Tubman, and I said I'd kiss you?" Maurice said.

Chelsea giggled. "Oh Maurice!"

Heston glared at Maurice. "Come on," he urged, "we'll all be late for school and we'll be in trouble." But Heston wasn't worried about being late. He liked Chelsea. Chelsea could see that. Heston didn't want Maurice messing with her.

Chelsea and Inessa pedaled on, and the boys jogged. Chelsea saw her friends around the statue of Harriet Tubman—Athena, Keisha, Falisha Colbert, the whole gang. She felt good. She felt free. She felt like anything was possible again.

"Hey Chel!" They were all shouting.

CHAPTER TWO

On Friday night, Jaris and his girlfriend, Sereeta Prince, double-dated with Oliver Randall and Alonee Lennox. They'd been to a movie. Now they were going down Grant Street looking for a new restaurant that had just opened up. Grant Street had a bad reputation, but a new Thai restaurant had leased a spot. The people were refugees, and they didn't have enough money for a pricey location. They were taking a chance on opening here. Their aim was to serve such good food that they would change the whole neighborhood.

Jaris and his friends had heard the food was amazing. And they wanted to support the first business in ages with the courage to open on Grant Street. The girls especially wanted to sample the Thai food, though Jaris and Oliver would have been just as happy with burgers and fries.

"Oliver's father ate there Sunday night with a friend," Alonee commented. "They had Thai chicken with basil. What else did your father say, Oliver?"

"The chicken had jalapeno chilies and garlic, chopped nuts, and coconut, all spread on top of the pieces," Oliver answered. "Dad and his friend freaked."

"You got me hooked," Sereeta responded, laughing.

Jaris pulled over between two parked cars to let a car go by in the opposite direction.

"Man," he commented, "they oughta make this one way or not let cars park in the street."

"You're right, Jare. It's narrow," Oliver noted.

Then they heard a popping sound, like firecrackers, but they all knew instantly that firecrackers weren't making the sound.

"Somebody shooting up the street," Jaris remarked grimly, with a terrible feeling in the pit of his stomach.

"Sounded like it's happening over at the apartments," Oliver added.

Hearing gunfire at the apartments on Grant, especially on the weekends, wasn't unusual. Chelsea's girlfriend, Sharon, told her that she had already seen four dead people lying near where she lived. All of them were under twenty.

Suddenly, out of the darkness, a bright white light appeared in the street directly ahead of Jaris's car. The light was very far away but coming head-on at them—and fast. The bright white light split into two headlights. A car was coming at them at high speed.

"Jaris," Sereeta screamed. She was sitting beside Jaris in the front seat of the Honda Civic. Oliver and Alonee were sitting in the back.

"Lookout!" Oliver yelled, putting his arms around Alonee. He pressed her face to his chest, preparing for the impact.

The headlights hurtled toward them on the narrow street, not slowing down at all. They got bigger and bigger. They were *close*! Jaris had never been so terrified in his life. A car-buckling head-on collision was only a heartbeat away. Jaris then saw a space between parked cars. He yanked the steering wheel sharply, bouncing the Honda between the cars, over the curb, and up onto a front lawn. As the dark sedan sped past, Jaris got a quick glimpse of the driver. They'd escaped a deadly collision by inches.

"Oh dear God!" Alonee cried. "That was close." She was trembling in Oliver's arms.

"He almost got us!" Oliver exclaimed. "Jaris, that was awesome driving, man. You saved our lives."

Sweat seeped through Jaris's T-shirt. He sat at the wheel, his head down, shaking. "I didn't know what else to do," he gasped. "I just had to get out of his way somehow . . ."

Sereeta reached over and grasped Jaris's hand. "Babe," she whispered in a trembling voice, "you saved all of us."

Everyone got out of the car. Oliver threw an arm around Jaris's shoulders, "You okay to drive, man? I'll take over for you if you want."

Jaris handed Oliver the car keys. His hand shook. "Thanks, man," he said.

Police sirens filled the night. They seemed to be going in the direction of the apartments, where the firecracker sounds came from.

Jaris climbed into the back seat of his Honda with Sereeta. "Something bad went down," he commented.

"Jaris," Sereeta whispered, "you were amazing. If you hadn't got out of the way, we'd all be in a twisted wreck now. We would've been hurt badly or maybe even dead. That guy who came at us. He wanted to get away from whatever happened over there. He was like crazy . . . Maybe, you know, he was the shooter or something."

Oliver carefully backed the Honda off the lawn, bounced over the curb into the street. Nothing seemed to be damaged.

"You'll probably need an alignment pretty soon," Oliver noted wryly. He glanced back at Jaris and Sereeta. Jaris was leaning back in the seat, his eyes closed. "I take it everybody has lost their appetite for Thai food," he suggested.

"I just want to go home," Alonee declared.

Sereeta nodded and agreed. "Me too. Wow, seeing that car coming dead ahead at us . . . I think I'm gonna have nightmares for weeks!"

Oliver somehow made a U-turn and headed the car back down the street, away from the apartments.

"Did anybody see the driver of that car?" Oliver asked as he drove. "At the speed he was going I doubt that—"

"I had my eyes closed," Alonee replied. "I thought we were all gonna die, and I didn't want to see it happen."

"I just saw a blur as he went by," Sereeta added. "But I think it was a guy at the wheel."

Jaris opened his eyes and spoke slowly, hesitantly. "I did see the driver. It was weird. As we bounced over the curb, I turned and looked at the car. You know, checking to see if we'd cleared the street so he wouldn't bang into the back of the car. I thought I . . . you know, recognized him."

"For real?" Oliver asked. "Who was it?"

"You know, I could be all wrong," Jaris cautioned, his eyes stills shut. "I was so panicky I can't trust what I saw, or felt. But it looked like Shane Burgess."

"Ms. McDowell's half-brother?" Oliver gasped. "Sparky? Oh Jaris, that'd be bad news. She's been making such progress with him."

"I'm not sure," Jaris protested. "I don't feel sure at all. I wouldn't want to even tell anybody 'cause I'm so unsure. It mighta been some dude who *looked* like Shane. It all happened so fast. The guy wore a stocking cap, a dark stocking cap pulled down, and you couldn't see much of his face."

Ms. Torie McDowell was everyone's favorite history teacher at Tubman High School. Jaris, Oliver, Alonee, and Sereeta were taking AP American History from her this year. She had a rough background and triumphed over it. Her little brother, Shane, was struggling with gang connections and drugs, and he lived at Ms. McDowell's condo. The last thing in the world Jaris wanted to do was to get Shane Burgess into trouble if he wasn't driving that car. Someone else could have been at the wheel.

Oliver checked the news on his iPhone. The police had cordoned off two blocks of Grant. Four young men had had a confrontation. Loud talk preceded shouting, and then shots rang out. One man was lying on the sidewalk. Police were not saying so, but he appeared to be dead.

"Oh brother!" Jaris groaned. "Bad, huh?"

"I just felt somebody had died. I could feel it in my bones," Alonee declared sadly.

"You guys," Jaris said, "don't anybody mention who I thought I saw driving that car. I'm so not sure. Okay?"

"Of course not," Sereeta agreed. "We were all so shaken up. And it happened so fast."

Oliver dropped off Sereeta and Alonee. By then, Jaris felt okay to take the wheel again. He had finally stopped shaking. He drove Oliver to his home.

"Well that stunk!" Jaris remarked bitterly. "We had a beautiful warm night with the moon shining. We go to have a little fun. Then the whole street explodes into a battlefield. Man, what's with this anyway?"

Oliver nodded. Oliver's father was over seventy, so he recalled gentler times. "You got that right, Jare," Oliver agreed. "Dad told me about the gangs that fought in his time up in Los Angeles. They fought with fists. Maybe some really bad dude had a knife. Now they all got guns, and, you're right, it's like war. Guys from one end of town got to go and kill dudes from another neighborhood or another school. And all that's just because—*what*? Some crazy gang creed. *That's* worth dying for?"

Oliver was still shaking his head. He got out of the car and headed for his front door.

Finally Jaris was alone in the car, heading home. He flipped on the car radio and got the local news. The announcer was saying that the coroner was on the scene over on Grant. Somebody had died all right.

When Jaris walked into his house, his parents were watching television.

"Hi sweetheart," Mom greeted. "Were you anywhere near Grant? We were worried."

"We were near there, Mom, but I didn't see what happened," Jaris replied. "We heard the shots."

"Lousy punks!" Pop fumed. "Killin' each other for amusement. What they got to fight over?"

Jaris's parents had grown up with gun violence as rampant as it was now. Pop had once said, "I musta been ten when I seen my first dead body, older kid from the neighborhood. Poor devil with half his head blown off. I'd seen him around the streets. One time on a hot day he bought me a cola. I didn't know his name, but he seemed all right."

"Chelsea told me her friend Sharon over on Grant has seen four dead guys already," Jaris remarked. "She's in the apartments on Grant. Everybody just expects it now."

"I wish they'd bring in the army," Pop declared. "The soldiers. I'd like to see them patrollin' the streets. When these punks show up with their drugs and their guns, throw 'em in the lockup for a good long time."

Pop bobbed his head at Jaris and Mom. "It's gettin' to be too much for the cops. They're outgunned by the punks now. Young cop a few months ago, the punks are lying in wait for him like snipers. He comes along and they take him down without even blinkin'. He didn't have a chance. Left a young wife and two babies. He looked like a kid himself. It ain't right. Somethin' gotta be done." Pop's voice was laced with bitterness.

"I really got scared when it came over the news about the shooting," Mom remarked. "I kept thinking about you guys being out there. I thought, 'What if they're caught in the crossfire or something?' I'm so glad you're home safe."

Jaris decided not to tell his parents about the near head-on accident. They didn't need to know that they saw a speeding car, maybe fleeing the crime—and almost killing them all. Nothing could be gained by describing the close call. Telling them would just add to their worry the next time Jaris was out with his friends.

As Jaris was walking to his room, Chelsea came from her bedroom. "I got all the news when it first broke, Jaris," she declared. "It happened over there where Sharon lives. She told me about the first dead guy she saw years ago, when she was about nine. It made her really scared. He was laying there, and they hadn't covered him up yet. Sharon said she had nightmares for a long time 'cause he was all bloody. But when she saw the next coupla dead guys, it didn't bother her as much. I wonder if she saw the guy who died tonight? Poor Sharon. I'm glad we don't live over there on Grant."

"Yeah, chili pepper," Jaris agreed. "Nobody should have to live where stuff like that happens. But, you know, it's not safe at night even around here. That's why Athena and her friends shouldn't be hanging at the twenty-four-seven store at night. Chili pepper, don't you ever hang with her when she does stupid stuff like that."

Chelsea nodded. "Athena told me she and Maurice Moore were out the other night. They peeked in the window of that abandoned house they call the ghoul house. I told her that was really stupid."

As Chelsea went to bed, she had a fleeting desire to have the kind of freedom that

Athena had. She wanted to be able to do whatever she wanted. But then, Chelsea thought, Athena's parents didn't love her as much as Chelsea's parents loved her. Chelsea decided in her heart she wouldn't trade parents for anything in the world.

Jaris went to bed thinking about Shane Burgess. He was an outstanding baseball player at Harriet Tubman High School when he was a sophomore. Everyone called him "Sparky" because of his fastball. Whenever Jaris saw him, he was wearing those red sneakers and oversized pants. He seemed like an okay kid, but something was wrong in his family.

Sparky's half-sister, Ms. McDowell, shared the story of her childhood with many students. She hoped to show them that, whatever the obstacles, they could survive and make good lives for themselves. Torie McDowell's parents died young of drug overdoses. The children had to fend for themselves. An older woman became a mentor for Ms. McDowell, rescuing her, but Shane descended into the life of street gangs and drugs. Now Ms. McDowell was providing a home for Shane and trying to keep him from rejoining the Nite Ryders, a local gang with its headquarters on Grant.

Right before he fell asleep, Jaris told himself that he had to have been mistaken. He couldn't have seen Shane escaping from the scene of a crime. Ms. McDowell was working too hard with the boy. He couldn't be in trouble again. And, if even by some odd coincidence, Shane *was* driving the car that almost hit them, he probably had nothing to do with the shooting. Maybe Shane had heard the shots and just wanted to get away fast.

At school on Monday, everybody at Tubman was talking about the Grant Street shooting. A young man had been shot to death. His name was Buster Bennett, and he was a student at Lincoln High School. He was sixteen years old, a pretty good student, and an outstanding football player.

Sadly, he had no known gang connections. He had gone over to Grant to visit a cousin who lived there. As far as anybody could tell, Buster was an innocent bystander. Buster was standing on the sidewalk, talking to his cousin. Then two guys that nobody knew supposedly drove up in a dark sedan. They started arguing with Buster's cousin. Then they pulled out guns and started firing before they took off in the car.

About a dozen people were in the front yard when the violence broke out. They all scattered quickly. They hid behind walls and ran into the apartments to escape the gunfire. Witnesses said the whole thing went down in a minute. One second Buster was talking to his cousin. The next second gunfire started, and he was down, fatally shot in the head.

Otherwise, the witnesses were of little help to the police. Maybe they were so frightened when the gunfire broke out that they didn't see anything. Or else they might have been too scared to tell the police what they saw. That was often how people reacted, especially when gangs were involved. If you talked to the police, you became a target yourself. Nobody wanted to get on the wrong side of the bad dudes who'd already committed murder.

Jaris stood by Harriet Tubman's statue with Alonee, speaking quietly. "They're saying the guys who did the shooting were driving a dark sedan, Alonee. That car that almost got us was a dark sedan."

"Yeah," Alonee said, nearly in a whisper. "I was so scared, I can't even say for sure what kind of a car it was. Maybe a Ford?"

"Maybe," Jaris replied. "All I remember are those lights comin' at us and expecting to die."

Later that day, they went to Ms. McDowell's AP American History class. You couldn't tell from Ms. McDowell's behavior whether she was worried about her brother. Maybe she didn't know what he was doing last night. Or maybe she had nothing to be worried about. Maybe the guy Jaris saw was somebody else.

After class, Jaris struck up a conversation with Ms. McDowell. "Is Shane playing baseball over at the school where he's going now, Ms. McDowell? I'll never forget what a great baseball player he was. He saved the day in that playoff game. After that, he was 'Sparky' to everybody."

Ms. McDowell smiled. "Yes, my brother was good at baseball, but he hasn't picked it up again. I hope he will." There seemed a note of concern in Ms. McDowell's voice. Jaris wasn't sure whether it was only his imagination.

"Well, as long as he's happy doing what he's doing," Jaris commented. "But he sure beat the Wilson Wolverines that day. We all cheered until we were hoarse."

Jaris had turned to walk away, when Ms. McDowell's voice stopped him. "Jaris, did you know anyone in that boy's family?" she asked. "The boy who died over on Grant? One of his cousins goes to school here at Tubman, you know. He's a senior, and I thought perhaps you knew him. Zendon Corman."

"Zendon Corman?" Jaris repeated the name. "The guy with the band? I've heard him play. His band's called After the Crash. I don't really know the guy, but some of my friends know him. They like his music."

Jaris thought about Carissa Polson, Kevin Walker's girlfriend. She had dated Zendon Corman for a while after she broke up with Kevin. Now she was with Kevin again. Jaris couldn't remember ever having a real conversation with Zendon. But seeing him from a distance, Jaris did not particularly like him. He seemed like a phony.

"I don't know the guy, Ms. McDowell," Jaris remarked. "But I've seen him around."

"A real tragedy!" Ms. McDowell sighed. "The waste of another young life in the neighborhood."

"Yeah," Jaris agreed.

That afternoon, Jaris happened to see Zendon walking across the campus. In all the time both boys had been students at Tubman, they exchanged small talk about the weather maybe twice. Jaris remembered being in the library once when Zendon was there. They talked briefly about the fire danger because the Santa Ana winds were blowing up. Now Jaris walked over to Zendon. He thought expressing his sympathy was the decent thing to do.

"I'm real sorry about your cousin, man," Jaris told him. "I just learned that Buster was a cousin of yours. From all I hear, he was a good guy. I'm real sorry."

Zendon nodded. He was a handsome guy. The girls went a little crazy over him when he performed with his band. To Jaris, he seemed to have a lot of ego. His band had a pretty good edgy sound, but Jaris didn't like it.

"Yeah, thanks," Zendon replied. "Man, it came out of nowhere."

Jaris was about to ask Zendon if he knew anything about who killed Buster. Then Zendon went on. "I was right there talking to Buster. We were gonna go for pizza when these gangbangers—I guess that's what they were—just wheeled up. They were packing heat, and it was all over in a few seconds. It just was crazy. It happened so fast it's just like a dream . . . a real bad dream."

CHAPTER THREE

That evening, the Spains sat down to one of Pop's great dinners. He'd made beef in spicy chili sauce.

Jaris," Chelsea asked, "did you ever see the ghoul house?"

"The *what*?" Jaris asked.

"You remember," she replied. "I told you Athena and Maurice went and peeked in one night. Don't you remember me telling you?"

"Maybe I didn't hear you," Jaris answered. "I musta been thinkin' of something else. What're you talking about, chili pepper?" Jaris helped himself to a big serving of Pop's beef in chili sauce.

"On our way to school, me and Inessa pass this house," Chelsea explained. "It's kinda green and broken down. It's got a brick wall in front. Inessa said she's heard weird sounds like screams comin' out of there. It's mostly shut up 'cause I guess the people who live there didn't pay their mortgage and the bank foreclosed."

"I don't remember ever seeing the place," Jaris responded.

Pop entered the conversation. "Little girl, don't go nosing around places like that. Maybe you and Inessa better ride your bikes on the other side of the street."

"Okay, Pop," Chelsea agreed.

"Sometimes homeless people camp in those foreclosed houses," Mom advised. "These people have nowhere to go. They see the empty house, and they think, 'Why can't we just go in?' At least they have a roof over their heads."

"Inessa said the screams sounded like you hear in a horror movie," Chelsea went on.

"Maybe the kids go in there and scream and holler just to scare people," Jaris suggested.

"Athena looked in one time," Chelsea finally admitted. "Athena said she saw skinny gray people walking around in there, but I don't believe her. Sometimes Athena makes stuff up."

"Sometimes Athena is a nut case," Pop declared. "Less you have to do with her the better, little girl. Enough bad stuff already goin' on in the neighborhood. Nobody needs her making up stories of skinny gray people sashayin' around. Athena's mom, that Trudy Edson, she gives me the willies. She needs to be watching that kid of hers."

Chelsea changed the subject.

"Keisha said the cousin of the boy who was killed over on Grant goes to Tubman," Chelsea reported. "I bet he feels really bad. His name is Zendon Corman. He's got a band and stuff."

"Yeah," Jaris added. "I talked to him today. I told him how sorry I was. I don't know the guy real well, but I thought I ought to say something."

"This Zendon," Pop asked, "he there when it happened?"

"Yeah," Jaris replied. "As a matter of fact, he was right there. He's like saying he coulda got shot too."

"I'm surprised the kid came to school after somethin' like that," Pop commented.

"There must have been a lot of witnesses," Mom added.

"You'd think," Pop agreed. "But at a time like that, people scatter and hide. Then they sorta forget they saw anything 'cause they don't wanna rat out gang members. Lot of these killings never solved 'cause nobody'll talk to the cops. Too bad too. Then there's just more killing."

"Zendon said he never saw the guys who took his cousin down before," Jaris said. "They just came along in this dark sedan and started yelling. The next minute, pop-pop-pop! And Buster Bennett was down. He was only sixteen. Seemed like a good kid too. An athlete, no gang ties."

"I bet the Nite Ryders were involved in this," Mom declared. "People think they're just innocent taggers, but they do a lot worse. Drugs, shootings. That's why I was concerned when Ms. McDowell brought her brother back into the neighborhood. He was a Nite Ryder once."

"Yeah, but the kid is doin' fine now," Pop said.

Jaris suddenly lost his appetite. He remembered the dark sedan hurtling toward them right after the shooting. In his mind, he could vaguely see the guy at the wheel who looked like Shane Burgess.

Jaris was glad when dinner was over, and he could slip off to his room. But he didn't quite make it. Chelsea was at his heels. "Can I talk to you, Jare?" she asked.

"Sure, chili pepper," Jaris agreed. But he was in no mood to hear about some girly jealousies and rivalries in the freshman class at Tubman. He didn't care who was talking to whom because of some imagined slight. But Chelsea looked upset. If something was really wrong, Jaris wanted to help.

Chelsea followed Jaris into his room. She sat on the edge of his bed while he sat down at the computer desk.

"Jaris," Chelsea confided, "I didn't want to say anything in front of Mom and Pop. You know how they feel about Athena, and some of the stuff she does."

"Yeah, chili pepper," Jaris replied wearily. "What's Athena up to now?"

"Well," Chelsea went on, "her and Maurice Moore went to the twenty-four-seven store again real late. Her parents weren't home."

"She shouldn't do that," Jaris advised. " Remember that time the bad dude tricked her into drinking liquor and she passed out? That was so dangerous."

"Yeah, I know," Chelsea admitted. "But today Athena told me something bad."

"What?" Jaris asked in a bored voice.

"It's about that Shane Burgess, Ms. McDowell's brother," Chelsea responded.

Jaris stiffened. His blood pressure went up. "What about Shane?" he demanded.

"Well, Athena and Maurice were going home," Chelsea told him. "And they saw Shane and Brandon Yates, and they were smoking dope."

Jaris felt a chill go up his spine. "Oh man, that's too bad, Chelsea," Jaris groaned. "I hate to hear that. Shane hangin' with Brandon and doing drugs. Ms. McDowell is such a wonderful lady. She's put her heart and soul into helping Shane."

"Maurice is real bold, Jaris," the little sister continued. "So he asked Shane what he was doing. Shane said he was a homie, and he didn't need no outsider on his turf. Shane said him and Brandon were Nite Ryders and Maurice better take off."

Chelsea glanced toward the door, as if to check that no one was eavesdropping.

"Shane was talking real tough," she went on. "He was saying he's not afraid of anything or anybody, not even the ghetto birds. Let 'em come, he said. Shane could see that Maurice was sorta taking all that in 'cause Maurice sorta admires guys like that. Sometimes Maurice acts like a wannabe gangbanger, but he won't ever do it. Shane offered him a smoke, but Maurice didn't take it. That's what Athena said anyway. I don't know if Athena is telling the truth. Sometimes she lies."

Jaris looked hard at his little sister. "Chili pepper, you listen to me, okay?" he commanded. "Don't be hanging too much with Maurice. Sounds like he's right on the edge. He thinks being a Nite Ryder is all macho and exciting. He's too young and stupid to know how it ends up. Sooner or later, some dude takes you down. Then you're lying in some alley choking on your own blood."

"You don't have to worry about me, Jaris," Chelsea assured him. "I don't like Maurice, but we let him eat lunch with us 'cause maybe having nice friends will sorta help him, you know? He wants to kiss me, but I'd punch him out if he tried."

When Jaris saw Oliver Randall in the morning, he told him about Shane. He said Shane was hanging with Brandon Yates and back with the Nite Ryders.

"What are we gonna do, man?" Jaris asked. "The kid's in trouble again. Maybe Ms. McDowell doesn't want to believe it, and she's just in denial or something. I hope that wasn't him I saw the other night driving that car. But even if it wasn't, he's on the skids."

Oliver looked grim. "Jaris," he declared, "we gotta tell Ms. McDowell what's going on. We gotta level with her. We owe her that."

Jaris and Oliver debated who should talk to Ms. McDowell. Oliver finally told Jaris that he had to do it because he was closer to the teacher. Oliver was a newcomer to Tubman. Ms. McDowell had a close relationship with Jaris, even relying on him in tough situations. One time he took over her class when she had to handle a bad situation on campus.

But the last thing Jaris wanted to do was bring Ms. McDowell this bad news. What he had to say about someone she desperately loved, her little brother, could be devastating.

"Hi, Ms. McDowell," Jaris said, nervously peering into the empty classroom. She was working at her desk.

"Hi, Jaris, come on in," she said with her usual smile. She was a very beautiful woman. About half the boys in her class had crushes on her. Of course, she was so totally professional that no problems ever developed.

"Ms. McDowell, I'm having a real hard time with this," Jaris admitted.

Ms. McDowell looked concerned. "Come on in and sit down, Jaris," she told him. Jaris took a chair near the teacher's desk.

"My little sister, Chelsea," Jaris began, "she told me something last night that made me feel sick. One of Chelsea's friends saw Shane and Brandon Yates in an alley smoking weed. They said they were Nite Ryders." Jaris blurted it all out.

Ms. McDowell was silent for what seemed like an eternity. Then she spoke. "Thank you for having the courage to tell me this, Jaris."

"I wanted you to have a heads-up, Ms. McDowell," the boy responded. "I didn't see it myself, so I can't be sure it's true."

"I understand, Jaris," the teacher replied. "Thank you so much." That was all she said. But a terrible sadness filled her eyes. Clearly, she already knew something was going wrong with her brother.

Jaris met Oliver some distance from Ms. McDowell's office. Then they went to the Coffee Camp for some cheap lattes.

"How'd she take it?" Oliver asked.

"I don't know, Oliver," Jaris answered. "She thanked me for telling her. But she's a smart lady. I think she already suspected the kid was in trouble again."

"You didn't say anything about the guy who almost hit us?" Oliver asked.

"No. I couldn't bring that up," Jaris replied. "It was such a quick look, I'm not sure it was Shane. I couldn't burden her with that. It wouldn't have been right when I'm so far from being sure."

That evening, the Spain family watched the latest news about the shooting. It was reported that police had put out a request for witnesses to come forward. A reward was offered for anybody who saw anything. Anonymous tips were welcomed. Tipsters didn't even have to give their names if they were afraid.

As they were watching, Jaris recalled that Chelsea's friend, Sharon, lived near the scene of the crime. Her mother had already called the police and told them what Sharon saw that night. Maybe, Jaris thought, Sharon would talk to him.

When the news was over, Jaris gave Chelsea a nod of his head. He was trying to send the message that he wanted to talk with her—privately. Chelsea's eyebrows crinkled in puzzlement for a second, then relaxed. Chelsea got the message and went down the hallway to her room. Jaris waited a beat and then followed her.

In her room, Jaris explained what he wanted.

"Chili pepper," he began, "your friend Sharon, she lives near where the shooting went down, right?"

"Yeah," Chelsea replied. "But she already went to the police. Her mom said they had to tell the cops what they saw. Sharon was looking out the window, and she heard this pop-pop noise. She said, 'I knew right away that somebody was shooting.'"

"Could you call her and see if she would tell me what she saw?" Jaris asked.

"Sure, Jare," the little sister said, dialing up her friend as she spoke.

Jaris took the phone from Chelsea.

"Hey, Chel," Sharon said.

"Sharon, this is Jaris, Chelsea's brother. My sister says you might tell me what you saw on Grant the other night."

"Oh, hi Jaris!" Sharon responded. "Sure! . . . Well, I heard the shooting, and then I heard the squealing, like a car going away real fast. It was a dark sedan. There were two guys in it, but I didn't see their faces or anything. Everybody was running. They were scattering like rabbits. All of a sudden I didn't see anybody except the dead guy lying there."

"Did you know any of the guys at the spot where it happened?" Jaris asked.

"I didn't see the fight break out," Sharon explained. "I just looked when the gunshots were going off. I saw Zendon, the guy who lives in the apartment across from us. The guy who got killed was his cousin. I saw Zendon runnin' just like everybody else."

"And you didn't see the shooters at all?" Jaris probed.

"Nah," Sharon answered. "They were outta there by the time I got to the window.

Mom said we gotta try to help the cops. If we don't, it's gonna just get worse and worse around here. I seen a lot of dead guys, Jaris. I get bad dreams. Sometimes the dead guys are alive again, and they're chasing me. Mom said we gotta try to help the police 'cause we all gonna die from the gangs if we don't."

Of course, Sharon and her mom were right. But that's not what Jaris was interested in. He asked, "Sharon, did you know the kid who was killed?"

"I saw him once or twice before," Sharon replied. "He was Zendon's cousin. He seemed okay. I see Zendon all the time, but his cousins don't come much. They live over by Lincoln."

At school the next day, Carissa Polson came to their lunch spot under the eucalyptus trees. Kevin wasn't with her because he had a meeting with Coach Curry.

"Awful thing for Zendon to be right there when his cousin went down, huh Carissa?" Destini asked.

"Yeah," Carissa agreed. "I'm glad I don't hang with him anymore. I'm so happy to be with Kevin again. I think those people on Grant are bad. I bet the guy who got killed was a drug dealer or something. I bet the fight was about drugs. Something about Zendon . . . I never really felt good about him."

"Probably somebody pay for a baggie and it was full of sand or something," Sami Archer suggested.

"What saves Zendon from bein' into the drugs and stuff is his music," Derrick Shaw commented. "He's so into his band that he's got no time for anything else."

"We almost got killed the night of the shooting," Jaris declared. "Me and Sereeta and Alonee and Oliver were driving around looking for this new Thai restaurant. Right after the shooting, this dark car comes right at us at a crazy speed. We didn't know if it was tied to the shooting, but it was coming at us—right at us. I thought we were gonna have a head-on collision and be killed."

"Whoa!" Sami cried. "What happened?"

Oliver smiled and explained. "Some of the most awesome defensive driving you ever want to see. The street was so narrow, there was nowhere to go. This dude here, Jaris, he threads the needle between two parked cars. He bounces the car over a curb and into some guy's front lawn. The car buzzed a few inches behind us. We had like less than a second to spare. He saved us all."

"That's true," Sereeta confirmed. "It still gives me the shakes thinking about how close we came."

"I wonder if the car that came at you was the murderers fleeing from killing that guy?" Carissa asked. "Did you recognize anybody in the car?"

Jaris exchanged a look with Oliver and answered. "It all happened really fast. I couldn't ID the guys. I don't even know the kind of car it was."

"You were probably eyeballing the killers, boy," Sami declared with a shudder.

Jaris felt nervous just talking about the incident. He changed the subject to Chelsea's ghoul house.

"Hey, anybody hear about the ghoul house?" he asked.

The kids in the group exchanged puzzled glances.

"My little sister," Jaris explained, "she's been telling me about a house on Navaho Street. It's an old rundown house the bank has taken over. She and her friends swore they heard screams coming from the house. This one kid, Athena—kind of an airhead—she peered in one day. She said she saw skinny gray people walking around in there. Sounds far-fetched. Athena is pretty weird herself, so maybe she made it up."

As Jaris was talking about the ghoul house, Kevin Walker arrived from his meeting. He was coming down the trail to the lunch spot under the eucalyptus trees. He grinned at Carissa and gave one of her braids a playful tug. Then he settled down with his lunch. He'd overhead Jaris talk about the ghoul house.

"I know the place you're talkin' about, Jaris," he began. "The boarded-up green dump on Navajo. I was jogging late at night once, and I heard these weird sounds coming out of there."

"Really?" Jaris said. So Athena and her friends weren't just making it all up.

"Yeah," Kevin affirmed. "I thought something strange was going on. I got closer and listened. I thought maybe somebody was being hurt in there. I like to mind my own business most of the time. But I'm not gonna ignore maybe a woman or a kid gettin' beat up by some freako. I was gonna call the cops, but then the front door opens."

All eyes were glued on Kevin. Everyone was looking at him that "and-then?" look.

Kevin continued. "This old guy is pushing a wheelchair with an old lady in it. He smiles at me and tells me the lady is his wife. She gets bad dreams, and she screams

58

out. Lady looked real nice, combed white hair. She even had pretty nice clothes. She kinda smiled at me too, but I could see that she was kinda confused. She asked me if I was her grandson Barry."

"You think that old couple lives in that abandoned house, Kevin?" Jaris asked.

"Well, he pushes her down the street," Kevin responded. "Then when they're out of sight, I go over there and look inside. It's pretty empty except for blankets on the floor. You can see somebody's camping in there."

"That's so sad," Carissa sighed. "Poor old people living like that."

"Yeah it is," Kevin agreed. "They're homeless people. We think all the homeless are guys with drugs and booze problems. Many of them are, but sometimes it's a family or old people. Lotta old people, they can't make it on their Social Security. Check the apartments. They cost the whole check the old guys get. Then there's nothing left over for food and the medicine that the Medicare, the government, doesn't cover."

"That's awful," Alonee remarked.

"It's a screwed-up world, Alonee," Kevin said.

"Somebody should do something," Alonee declared.

Kevin sneered. He liked Alonee. Everybody did. But Kevin thought she was a cockeyed fool sometimes.

"Alonee," he asserted, "nobody's gonna do anything. They all got their own problems. All we can do is leave those old folks alone. They got a lousy abandoned house to live in. When it rains, they aren't getting' wet, right? Before they found this dump on Navaho, they were probably sleeping in an abandoned TV carton behind a building. Maybe they'll get rousted tonight or maybe not. What we need to do is look the other way. They're doin' the best they can. If the authorities come around, they'll stick the old lady in a nursing home. Then they'll be separated. All they got is each other, and I'm not messing with that."

CHAPTER FOUR

Oh no!" Jaris moaned when he removed the birthday invitation from under his windshield wiper. "Oh man, no!" He'd been invited to a surprise birthday party for Jasmine Benson. The handwriting on the invitation made it clear who was setting up the party at Jasmine's house. Marko Lane was behind it.

The invitation read:

> The most beautiful, hottest chick at Tubman High School is turning eighteen. I know you'll want to be there to wish her all the happiness she deserves. She was the sweetest seventeen, and now she'll be the most stunning eighteen. Catch the biggest, most amazing birthday party in the hood or regret it for the rest of your natural life.

The date and time were at the bottom of the invitation. It was 7:30 the Friday after next.

"Oh brother!" Jaris muttered to himself. "This is just what I needed."

It was the end of the school day. He was in the Tubman parking lot, waiting for Sereeta. They were going to try again to make it to that Thai restaurant. Alonee and Oliver were going to meet them there.

"Babe," Jaris announced when Sereeta came walking along, "you will never guess what I just got invited to."

Sereeta grinned. "Mine came to me in English class," she replied waving a similar invitation in the air. "Like I would miss this for the world. I'd rather go dancing with a grizzly bear than go to this party."

"So what are you gonna do, Sereeta?" Jaris asked her. Sereeta rolled her eyes. "Go, of course, because I'm an idiot."

"Babe," Jaris asked gloomily, "why did we get these invitations? I'm not a friend of Jasmine's. It must be another of Marko's dirty tricks, to force us to buy her a gift."

"I never hung out with the girl in my life," Sereeta remarked, getting in the car. "She's always making snide remarks to me. Why would I want to be a part of her birthday party? But Jaris, we got the invitations because Marko must think we care about her. It'd be cruel to ignore them and say we don't care and aren't coming. I mean, I can't be cruel, no matter how sick this makes me."

Jaris got behind the wheel of the car, and they headed for the Thai restaurant. Prices were cheaper before the regular dinner hour.

"But babe," Jaris groaned, "Marko *must* know how we feel. He's not dumb."

"See," Sereeta explained, "it's like this. Jasmine has only a few real friends, if any. When that Princess of the Fair contest was held, Jasmine was sure she was going to win. She tried so hard to win that she pulled every trick in the book. She pretended to be a humanitarian collecting for poor kids, she passed out flowers. She turned off everybody in the school. Remember?"

Jaris nodded yes. "So," Sereeta went on, "Marko wants to give her a birthday party, and who is he gonna ask? Strangers on the street who don't know her? If he only gave invitations to kids who really liked him and Jasmine, nobody'd be there. Like, what if he gave a party and nobody came? So he decides to stick people like us with invitations 'cause he figures we wouldn't flat out hurt Jasmine by not coming. He knows us better than we know ourselves, babe."

"Yeah, you're right," Jaris granted.

Alonee and Oliver were already seated in the Thai restaurant when Sereeta and Jaris walked in.

"Hey!" Jaris hailed the couple.

"Hey yourself, dude," Oliver replied.

Jaris and Sereeta sat down, and Jaris immediately pulled out the unwanted invitation. "Is this my unlucky day or what?" he lamented. "Marko Lane's giving a birthday party for Jasmine and look—"

"Join the club," Oliver responded, producing his own invitation.

"Me too!" Alonee added glumly.

Oliver laughed. "Alonee has no right to complain. She's so nice that, of course, Marko would expect her to come and celebrate Jasmine's birthday. But Jaris, haven't we tried to kill Marko a couple times?"

"I bet Kevin won't get an invitation," Jaris commented. Last year, Kevin was about to beat the life out of Marko. At the last moment, Kevin heard his dead mother telling him not to do it.

"Maybe not," Oliver agreed. "But Kevin never laid a hand on Marko. I don't think Marko ever found out how close he came to dying. Who knows?"

"I bet Derrick'll get lucky," Jaris suggested. "His chick rally hates Jasmine. Jasmine really messed up Destini's life telling lies about her to her stupid boyfriend at the time. Surely Derrick'll escape the curse of the invitation."

"Nope, wrong!" Sereeta cut in. "When I was walking to your car Jaris, poor Derrick was holding a piece of paper in his hand like it was a scorpion. He held it away from his body, like it would bite him. He kept saying, over and over, 'Why me?' And Destini, being loyal to Derrick, she'll have to come too."

"Then who *didn't* get an invitation?" Jaris wondered aloud, shaking his head.

"Well, for sure Sami Archer and Matson Malloy got one," Sereeta figured. "Sami was really nice to Jasmine, especially when Jasmine and Marko broke up. Sami offered a shoulder to cry on to Jasmine, remember? So Sami's hooked."

"I wonder," Jaris mused, "if Marko sent an invitation to that homeless man who hit him over the head with the baseball bat. Remember, Marko knocked the guy's shopping cart into the gully?"

All four of them laughed.

"Jasmine's folks have a real nice house," Sereeta said. "I've never been there, but it looks great from the outside. It's nicer than most houses in the neighborhood. I bet everything'll be really decorated."

"And Marko'll hire a disc jockey or maybe even a live band," Oliver added. "He'll hit on his dad for money for the bash. The old man adores Marko. His only son. His grand progeny. Marko can do no wrong."

"I bet he hires Zendon," Jaris guessed. "That band, After the Crash, is pretty hot now. A lot of girls are freakin' over that dude. Personally, I don't like the guy, but that's me."

"I saw Zendon at school today," Sereeta said. "He was buying a soda pop for some girl. He was laughing and hanging all over her. It's amazing that he was right there when his poor cousin got wasted. How can he blow it off like that? You'd think he'd be feeling pretty bad or at least shook up. If I was standing near somebody who got murdered, I think I'd be shaking for a week. I was going to go over and offer my sympathy. Then it seemed just stupid the way he was acting."

"I guess he and his cousin weren't very close," Jaris suggested. "Zendon is a shallow dude anyway. He lured Carissa into that stupid relationship, making trouble between her and Kevin. Then, when she dumped him, he didn't care."

"I'm so glad Carissa and Kevin made up," Alonee remarked. "It's so cute when he runs and she's there again, yelling 'Go Twister!' She's made a big change in Kevin. He really likes Carissa. He was missing her something awful, even though he was too proud to show it."

"Kevin's got a really good heart," Jaris noted. "How many of us woulda reached out to Lydell Nelson like he did? He really got the guy to act like a human being instead of an obnoxious loner. Kevin pulled Lydell out of his shell. Lydell seemed to really blossom after that. And, you know, when we were all talking about that ghoul house, Kevin told us what he did. When he heard the screams, he went right in there to make sure nobody was getting hurt. Kev is hotheaded and aggressive, but he's really good in his soul. I like the guy a lot."

"Yeah," Oliver agreed. "Like that time Marko ridiculed my dad and I almost took Marko on. Kevin grabbed my arm and stopped me. He hardly knew me then, and yet he knew I was making a horrible mistake. He knew he could stop me from going over the line, and he did. I'll never forget that."

Oliver frowned then. "And now that creep Marko Lane is getting us all trotting off to the stupid birthday party for Jasmine. He'll be there swaggering around. It's gonna be Marko's show, and we're gonna have to be his loyal subjects. It burns me up, but what can we do?"

"Wow!" Sereeta exclaimed. "This chicken is really good."

The conversation turned to how good the food was. "Yeah, mine's great too." "Man, this stuff is super." And then the group fell silent while they ate.

After few minutes, Jaris said, "I sure wish they'd catch the creep who killed Buster Bennett. And I hope to heaven it doesn't have anything to do with Shane Burgess. Ms. McDowell is such a good person. It makes me sick, the kind of heartache she'd feel if her brother was mixed up in something really awful."

"Yeah," Oliver agreed. "I guess Shane is with the Nite Ryders again. His sister could pull him out of that as long as he hasn't done anything . . . you know, real bad."

"I hope he isn't strung out on drugs," Alonee commented. "Most of the Nite Ryders are."

Sereeta sighed. "I know Shane has had a rough start in life, but having a sister like Torie McDowell is so awesome. I can't believe she won't pull him through in the end. She loves him so much."

"I guess sometimes love isn't enough," Oliver remarked.

The next day at school, Trevor Jenkins came to Jaris by the statue of Harriet Tubman. "Jaris, can you beat this?" he asked bitterly. "Marko's treated me like a dog. Now he gives me an invitation to his girlfriend's birthday celebration. Man, I freaked out. He's a rat, and she's not much better. Remember when he ratted me out to my ma that I had a girlfriend—just to make trouble for me? Dude, this is like a bad joke!"

"You don't have to go, Trevor," Jaris suggested.

"I bet you're going, Jare," Trevor replied. "I know you got stuck with one of these stinkin' invitations too. You're going even though Marko's hurt Sereeta, yelling about her mom's problems. Man, are we supposed to forget all that stuff and make like nothin' ever happened?"

"I wouldn't go if it was a birthday party for Marko," Jaris admitted. "I just wouldn't. But Jasmine, she's a chick. I can't hurt her like that. There'd she be sitting in her empty house, bawling her head off. I can't get my brain around that, man."

"Yeah," Alonee added. "She's a human being."

Derrick appeared then. "Who's a human being?" he asked. Destini was just behind him.

"Jasmine Benson," Alonee answered.

"That's not what I heard," Derrick said, his frown deepening. "I mean, she's been awful cruel sometimes. It's gonna be so hard for Destini to come."

"I'll go for you, babe," Destini offered. "But I'll be grinding my teeth the whole time."

"How could Marko think we *want* to come to this?" Derrick asked, a bewildered look on his face.

"He knows we don't want to come," Jaris explained. "But we're stuck, and he knows that. She's a seventeen-year-old chick, and she's gotta know nobody likes her. But if we skunk her by boycotting her party, she's gonna remember that for the rest of her life. All her classmates at Tubman hated her so much they wouldn't spend two hours at a dumb party for her birthday. I'm not puttin' that on any chick, even Jasmine. I'm not letting her know we all hate her that much. No way."

"But we do hate her," Destini declared.

"You guys do what you think is right," Jaris suggested wearily. "But Sereeta and me are going."

"Me and Oliver too," Alonee said. "After all, how bad can it be? A couple hours, and we're outta there."

"Yeah," Derrick admitted, looking nervously at Destini. "Okay, babe?"

Destini smiled and kissed Derrick. "For you babe, I'd go to Dracula's birthday party."

After morning classes, they all gathered under the eucalyptus trees for lunch. Jasmine's party had become the number one topic, even more than the recent murder on Grant.

"What'll I get her for her birthday?" Jaris asked nobody in particular. "We gotta get her gifts too."

Kevin was there with Carissa. He had not received a birthday invitation. Now he lay on the grass with his head in Carissa's lap. "A poisoned apple?" he mused. "After all, she's a witch, and maybe she'd like a poisoned apple."

Carissa giggled wildly.

"Soap maybe," Jaris suggested desperately. "Girls like sweet smelling soap, right?"

"No," Sereeta objected. "We're very particular about the scents we like. If you get the wrong scent, she'll just have to throw it out."

"So, who cares?" Kevin asked. "Maybe as she's throwing it, Marko'll come walking by, and she'll hit him in the head."

"Perfume," Oliver declared. "Chicks like perfume."

"That's worse than soap," Sereeta objected. "People are very partial to their favorite scents. Certain scents even give people terrible headaches."

"Hey," Kevin cut in, "now we're getting somewhere. Find the one that'll give her a headache."

"Stop it, Kevin," Sereeta laughed.

"Oh man!" Jaris grumbled.

"I know," Destini said. "Let's get her a subscription to *Mean Girls* magazine."

"Is there such a thing?" Derrick asked hopefully.

"No," Kevin said, "but there should be for chicks like Jasmine."

The group chuckled for a second but then gave up on gift ideas.

"You guys hear anymore about the shooting over on Grant?" Kevin asked. "I sorta knew that dude who was killed. When we had the last track meet at Lincoln, I met Buster Bennett. We talked about the NFL. He was a nice guy. We talked about how we strengthen our legs for our sports. I liked him. Too bad a good kid like that had to catch lead. But ain't it always the way?"

"Probably some fight started at Lincoln during the day," Alonee suggested, "and they finished it over at his cousin's house on Grant. That often happens. Lotta times guys start fighting at school. Then, when it gets dark, they start up again, this time for real. Might've even been over a girl. Maybe Buster Bennett tried to date somebody else's chick, and the boyfriend got him. Maybe Buster stole some girl from another guy, and this was revenge."

"Yeah," Kevin commented, grinning at Carissa. "I coulda wasted Zendon when he took you from me, babe."

"But you wouldn't have killed him," Carissa said.

"Who knows?" Kevin crowed, then he laughed.

When Jaris got home, he told his parents about the birthday party for Jasmine Benson. "We were all shocked when we got the invitations," Jaris grumbled. "Marko knows how we all feel."

"That Marko character throwin' the bash, Jaris?" Pop asked.

"Yeah, he's behind it, but it's going to be at Jasmine's parents' house," Jaris replied. "Nobody likes Jasmine, but now we gotta get her a gift and go to the party."

"So don't go," Pop advised. "Ain't no law says you gotta go to a party where you don't wanna be. This Marko Lane's a creep. He's been creepy since he was knee-high to a grasshopper. Jasmine, she's always on his side, so they're a crummy pair. Stay away."

"No, Lorenzo," Mom objected. "That would be terrible. Jasmine's parents will be there. She's their only child. Can you imagine how they'd feel with a big party set up, tons of food, the balloons hanging all around, and nobody came? They'd be heartbroken."

"I don't like the Bensons anyway," Pop responded. "They raised a selfish little diva in that Jasmine. She don't deserve no party."

"You must go, Jaris," Mom declared firmly. "The Bensons are part of our community. We see them at Tubman at all the open houses and events like that. I'd feel awful if you snubbed them like that."

"Hey, Monie," Pop suggested, "I got an idea here. Why don't *you* go? You could dress up in your old school clothes from twenty years ago and just show up at the party. Maybe you could be carrying a balloon! The kid here don't want to go, and you're all for it. So *you go*."

"As usual, you are being ridiculous, Lorenzo," Mom told him. "Jaris, buy her some nice stationery, maybe with flowers embossed on it. Give it to her, and be at the party."

"No, Mom," Jaris said. "she doesn't use paper to write on. She tweets and texts. Most of the kids at school wouldn't know what to do with stationery."

"Dear me!" Mom exclaimed. "The world is passing me by. The next thing you know I'll be as old-fashioned as a horse and buggy. I feel so ancient and out of touch."

"Don't worry, babe, you're still hot to me. Always will be," Pop told her.

Chelsea now joined in the conversation. "You could get Jasmine a little doll, Jaris, like Barbie. Only make her mean-looking and dressed like a witch."

"Chelsea!" Mom scolded. "Jaris is not going to do something mean and spiteful like that."

"My enemy at school, Kanika," Chelsea explained, "she's having a birthday party soon. Athena and I are gonna get her sour-ball candy 'cause she's so mean."

Jaris sighed. "Kevin's lucky. He didn't get an invitation."

"So this bum Marko gonna be having a birthday party for himself when he turns eighteen?" Pop asked.

"His father'll give him a big bash down-town or something," Jaris answered. "Marko isn't stupid enough to think we'd come to *his* party. That's why he's making such a big deal out of Jasmine's party. In a way he figures it's his party too."

"How about some nice fashion jewelry for Jasmine?" Mom suggested, still deeply involved in doing the right thing. "You can get it really cheap at Lawson's. They've got these pretty clunky beads the girls seem to be wearing. She can wear it over a nice top. It really dresses it up."

"Yeah, Mom," Jaris replied. "That's a good tip. Cheap huh?"

"Very inexpensive," Mom affirmed.

"Me and Sereeta can go there after school tomorrow," Jaris said. "We'll pick something out."

As Jaris was heading for his bedroom, Chelsea followed him.

"Jare," the girl said in a hushed voice, "Sharon called. Somebody got the license number of that car that drove away from Grant that night. Somebody on the street decided to call the cops and tell them. They were scared to do it before, but then they did. I think it was Sharon's grandmother.

She's a nice lady but she's so scared for her kids and grandkids."

"That's good, chili pepper," Jaris responded. "She did her duty."

Jaris felt a heaviness in his chest as he sat down at the computer. He hoped against hope that this wasn't the beginning of the end of Shane Burgess. What if he was in that dark sedan that sped from the murder scene? What if Jaris had been right in thinking he saw Shane at the wheel? Then it was only a matter of time that heartbreak would come to Ms. McDowell.

Did the license plate number belong to Shane Burgess? Jaris rebelled against the thought that Ms. McDowell's struggles to save her little brother could come to this. She was so strong, so brave, in how she triumphed over her own past. She lost her parents to drugs. She lost other siblings to the street. She lost her childhood to the dark world of the drug-infested streets. It wasn't fair, after all that, that she would now lose her brother too.

CHAPTER FIVE

Chelsea, Athena, Falisha, Keisha, and Inessa were eating their lunch in their favorite spot under the pepper trees.

"I found out about the ghoul house," Chelsea announced. "My brother's friend told Jaris all about it, and Jaris told me."

"What's the scoop?" Athena asked.

"Some old homeless people are hiding in the house," Chelsea explained. "They got no place else to stay, except maybe before they lived in a carton that a TV set came in. The lady gets scared sometimes, and she screams. I guess she has bad dreams or something."

"We should tell the police or something," Inessa said. "It's not right for people to be staying in a house when they don't pay rent or anything. That's cheating."

"But they got no place else to go," Chelsea objected. "Kevin, he's my brother's friend, he said to just leave them alone."

"We could like leave a bag of oranges or something," Athena suggested. "We could leave the bag on the steps. I bet they'd like that."

"Athena!" Chelsea cried. "That's a great idea! Let's do that tomorrow on our way to school."

"You know what Shad does?" Falisha asked.

Shad was Shadrach, a war veteran. He lost his eye, and his face was badly scarred by an IED in Iraq. Shadrach ran an opossum rescue center, and he had been dating Falisha's mother for some time. At first Falisha hated the idea of Shadrach and her mother being friends, but now she sorta liked Shadrach. Falisha's mother, Ms. Colbert, taught science at Tubman High to the freshman class.

"Shad gets these little packets of tuna," Falisha explained, "you know, with crackers in the package. They don't need to be refrigerated. He gives them out to the homeless people. He gives them little cartons of pudding too. I bet if we pooled our money, we could get a basket of stuff for the homeless old people. I bet Shadrach would help us."

"Way to go, Falisha," Athena cried.

"I don't know," Inessa objected. "My parents tell me to stay away from those homeless people. Maybe we shouldn't get involved. I mean, most of them are dangerous."

"I'm kinda scared of them too," Keisha admitted.

"We'll just collect the stuff, and Shadrach will deliver it," Falisha suggested. "I know he'd be happy to do that. He's really generous."

Athena opened her purse. "I got three dollars right here. I got more money for lunch and stuff, so I can kick in three dollars."

Chelsea looked in her purse. Grandma Jessie had sent her a nice money gift when she started freshman year. Chelsea felt guilty when she got the gift because she wasn't very nice to Grandma on her last visit. Grandma had suggested that Chelsea go away to a ritzy boarding school because Grandma thought Tubman was not a good enough school. Chelsea was so horrified at the thought of leaving her family and all her friends that she blew up at Grandma Jessie. But her grandmother sent her the money anyway. Now Chelsea put five dollars in the envelope they were passing around.

Inessa didn't open her purse. "We give money at church and that's enough," she declared.

Falisha added two dollars, and Keisha put in two dollars.

"Wow, we got twelve dollars," Chelsea announced. "When my mom goes grocery shopping tonight, I'll ask her to buy some of those tuna and pudding things and some oranges. You can give the basket to Shadrach to give to the old people, Falisha."

"Shadrach delivers me to school sometimes," Falisha said. "He brings Mom too. I'll give him the basket tomorrow morning. Wow! He can take it over to the old homeless people right away."

Inessa seemed disapproving. "I think this is all a big mistake." Inessa thought that homeless people and strange-looking people ought to be avoided because they were dirty and dangerous.

But Chelsea thought that some very nice-looking people could be dangerous too. Down on Grant the other day, the guys who killed poor Buster Bennett were probably nice-looking. They were probably clean and handsome, and maybe they even wore gold chains around their necks.

Chelsea wasn't mad at Inessa for not kicking in money for the basket. That's how Inessa was, and Chelsea still liked her. But Chelsea felt sad for her. What they were doing for the old homeless couple made

Chelsea feel very good and happy. Inessa felt sorry for her friends when something was wrong in their lives. But she couldn't feel sympathy for strangers.

Chelsea walked alone toward her next class. Her friend Sharon fell in step beside her. Sharon took the bus from Grant to Tubman High school every day. She wasn't dressed nearly as nicely as Chelsea's other friends, but she was clean and neat.

The girls exchanged greetings and continued to walk. Out of nowhere, Sharon started to confide in Chelsea.

"Chelsea, this shooting's got me spooked," Sharon confessed. "I got nightmares, Chelsea. Every night I hear that pop-pop sound, and I cover my ears. I pull the pillow over my head 'cause I think they're shooting again. I'm so scared. I mean, I've seen dead guys before, but this one was different. He was different, Chelsea. He was . . ." Sharon swallowed hard. "He was cute."

"Kevin, my brother's friend," Chelsea responded, "said he was nice too, Sharon. He played football. Kevin talked to him once when Kevin went to a track meet at Lincoln. They talked sports stuff. Kevin liked him. . . . I wonder why he was killed?"

"You know what, Chel?" Sharon asked. "Everybody in that family is so handsome. Some families, everybody lookin' okay, but those people all handsome. Zendon is so handsome that all the girls go crazy over him, especially when he plays his music. And Buster, he was the same way. He looked like some actor."

Sharon paced alongside Chelsea and stared hard at the ground. She continued. "He was lying there, and they hadn't covered him up yet. I looked at him. I shouldna looked. He had on a white T-shirt, and he had these big muscles. He only sixteen years old, Chelsea. That's two years older than us, and he's done for already. Don't seem right."

Chelsea looked at the other girl. Tears were in Sharon's eyes. "I never saw a dead person like that, Sharon," Chelsea admitted. "My uncle, I saw him in a casket at the funeral parlor. But he was old. He looked so peaceful, almost like he was smiling. I never saw somebody dead in the street like that. My brother's friend, Derrick, he saw a dead guy who'd been murdered. He was scared for a long time. I never want to see somebody who's been murdered."

"It's bad on Grant, girl," Sharon said. "Seem like they come there to deal drugs and settle their scores. I wish I didn't live in the apartments there."

When Pop had gotten home on Friday, he'd told Jaris he had to invite Sereeta over for Sunday dinner.

"You say the girl likes Asian food, Jaris?" Pop asked. "I'm makin' somethin' special on Sunday. It's not your Chinese or your Thai food. It's from Japan. Yeah. Called *shabu shabu*. It's got mushrooms, shrimp, mussels, scallops, veggies, the whole deal."

Pop grinned proudly over at Mom, who was finishing her computer work for her classes. "Way better," he declared, "than those meals you used to like to put out, babe—those whatchamacallit chicken nuggets or something in the cardboard boxes. Hard to tell where the cardboard ended and the chicken began."

Mom frowned. She was always so busy teaching that she had always relied heavily on frozen dinners in the plastic containers. Pop never let her forget it. Since he was cooking more and more for the family, they were enjoying much better food—fresh cooked. "Remember the turkey meal, you guys?" Pop chuckled. "It said there on the package that it was turkey. But that was the sorriest bird ever got tucked in a carton."

Chelsea giggled.

"Well, anyway," Pop said, grinning slyly, "you ask your girl over for Sunday dinner, Jaris. She'll get a kick out of this here *shabu shabu.*"

"Thanks, Pop, I will," Jaris agreed. He had told Sereeta about his dad's new cooking hobby. Sereeta loved Jaris's family. She thought the world of Chelsea, and she envied Jaris his wonderful parents. Sereeta especially enjoyed Pop's wild and unpredictable ways.

So now, on Sunday afternoon, Jaris and his parents were having Sereeta for Sunday dinner. Sereeta had driven to the Spains' house in her grandmother's car.

When she arrived, she was so excited about solving a big problem that she didn't wait to make her announcement.

"Jaris, I got a gift for you to give Jasmine!" she declared. She held up a box with pretty necklace in it. "I hope it's okay, Mrs. Spain. It's kinda blue wooden beads and stuff."

"Oh, it's lovely!" Mom responded. "Jasmine will love it. That is very kind and thoughtful of you to get it."

Sereeta appreciated Mom's support. But, despite the gift problem being solved, Jaris was still not a happy person.

"I got her a belt," Sereeta went on. "She likes belts for her jeans with sparkly stuff on them."

"I dread the party," he said to no one in particular. "I hope there's enough people there so Sereeta and I can sneak out early without being noticed."

"Jaris, don't do anything that's hurtful," Mom commanded.

"Yeah, boy!" Pop added. "Jasmine, she's hurt everybody at school a couple hundred times. But don't do nothin' to ruffle her little feathers."

Mom shot a look at Pop, who looked away from her. He shifted back and forth on his feet for a short second. Then he hit on a way to divert everyone's attention.

"Okay, everybody," he announced. "Dinner's ready. Let's all sit down."

Pop had arranged slivers of green onion, peeled sliced carrots, fresh spinach, and mushrooms on a tray. On another tray he placed the seafood. Then he put chicken broth on to boil, adding sherry, ginger, and soy sauce. When Sereeta walked in, the fondue pot was on the table, filled with simmering broth. They all chose whatever vegetable or seafood they wanted and put it into the broth for about four minutes to cook.

"This is amazing!" Sereeta gasped. "Mr. Spain, you're a master chef!"

Pop enjoyed the compliment mightily. He chuckled and turned to Jaris. "Boy, you picked a winner here. You wanna keep this girl. Beauty, brains, the works. You hit the old jackpot."

After the meal, when Sereeta was getting ready to leave, she spoke to Pop. "That was the most awesome Asian meal I have ever had, Mr. Spain."

Jasmine's birthday party was scheduled to begin at seven-thirty on Friday. Jaris picked Sereeta up at her grandmother's house. They arrived at the Benson home at seven thirty-eight. Quite a few cars were already there. Jaris figured that, if not enough people promised to come, Marko probably hired strangers to fill in. But then Jaris recognized some of the cars parked along the driveway and in the street. Oliver and Alonee had come in the BMW of Oliver's dad. Trevor had come in his brother's car. Sami Archer's mother had dropped off Sami, Matson, Derrick, and Destini.

"Look at all the balloons," Jaris noted as they got out of his Honda. A jungle of blue and gold balloons sprouted from the trees and shrubbery all around the big house. Some were hanging from the eaves of the house as well.

As Jaris opened the door for Sereeta, who was carrying their two packages, he commented, "Well, here goes nothing."

"Maybe we can cut out early," Jaris hoped.

Sereeta laughed, "We're not even inside yet, babe!"

The music was already playing, a mixture of rock and reggae. As Jaris suspected, Zendon and his After the Crash band were providing the entertainment. They were on an improvised stage in the big living room, banging away on their instruments.

Marko was at the door, welcoming the guests.

"Hey, Sereeta, you're lookin' hot, girl," he cried, beaming. "You lookin' pretty good too, dude. You got to see our birthday girl. She's in a blue sequined dress with a v-neckline. She's amazin'!"

"Wonderful,'" Jaris thought to himself. The smile he was forcing on his face was already painful. He spotted Jasmine moving among the guests. She *did* look beautiful. Jaris had to admit she was one of the most beautiful seniors at Tubman High, though Jaris thought Sereeta had her beat. Still, a lot of the guys at the party were doing double takes on Jasmine in her close-fitting dress. It was short, and it showed off her great legs. She wore super-high heels, making her even more striking.

Jaris put their gifts down on the already formidable pile of gaily colored packages. Alonee and Oliver looked over. Their body language indicated they were as eager as Jaris and Sereeta to make an early exit.

Zendon was starting a new set, and he held the microphone in his hand. In his dark, velvety voice, he crooned, "I want to dedicate this song to the beautiful young lady who is just turning eighteen. Jasmine Benson, this is for *you*, sweetheart."

Jasmine gave an excited little gasp and drew near the stage. Her gaze was fixed on Zendon, who looked unusually handsome in a striking red jacket.

Zendon delivered a tender ballad in a croon that departed from his rock music style.

> If all the stars turned dark, if all the
> sunlight failed,

Your smile would be enough to light the
world, my love.

Zendon sang in a warm, soft tenor. Jasmine continued to stare at him, as if enchanted. Jaris thought to himself that Marko was not a bad-looking dude. But Zendon was way better looking.

You are all I ever wanted, all I ever
needed . . .

Zendon sang with deep intensity, as if he meant every word. Jasmine was transfixed. Her large, beautiful eyes widened still more. She was so emotionally moved that she grasped her upper arms and seemed to tremble.

If you should go away, there's nothing left
to say.

Zendon crooned, clutching his guitar, which seemed to moan along with his voice.

You are my hopes and dreams, you are all I
ever wanted,

All I ever needed, angel of my nights,
Princess of my days, the one whose beauty
   lights
The dark and winding ways.

Jaris glanced over at Marko. He didn't look happy. Jaris nudged Sereeta and whispered, "I think Marko figures the dude's going too far."

"He looks like he's coming on to Jasmine," Sereeta remarked worriedly, sensing that the situation was about to deteriorate—badly.

Jasmine drew closer to Zendon, who finished the song with a flourish of guitar riffs. Zendon then reached out and took Jasmine's hand, kissing it fervently. Then—impulsively—Zendon took Jasmine in his arms and kissed her on the mouth. Jasmine was so moved, she seemed about to faint.

"Ohhhh! Bad move, dude!" Jaris groaned.

"Happy birthday, beautiful!" Zendon whispered into the microphone, oozing charm.

"Oh, thank you!" Jasmine gasped. "Oh, this is the most exciting moment of my whole life!"

Marko was pushing through the guests. He was shoving people aside in his haste to reach Jasmine. When the guests were arriving, Marko had been all smiles. Now he looked in deep distress. Some feeling that was close to horror twisted his face. Marko grabbed Jasmine's hand and dragged her away from the stage. He thrust her in front of Alonee and Oliver.

"These guys want to wish you a happy birthday, baby," Marko told her, though Alonee looked surprised. She had no special desire to talk to Jasmine.

Alonee had put her little gift on the pile and was edging toward the door. But, with Jasmine dragged before her, she smiled lamely. "Happy birthday, Jaz," she said. "Boy, what a party. Great party."

"Wonderful balloons too," Oliver added. "Uh, you look great, Jasmine. Really great. You bet."

"Wasn't that an amazing song Zendon sang to me," Jasmine sighed dreamily. "Zendon is magnificent!"

"Yeah, yeah, he's good," Marko admitted, still keeping a firm hold on Jasmine's arm. He didn't want her to escape back to the stage and flirt with Zendon again. "Other people want to wish you a happy birthday, girl. Come on."

"Let go of me, Marko," Jasmine snapped. "I needed to say something to Zendon. I didn't thank him properly for writing that beautiful song just for me."

"No, he didn't write it for you, babe," Marko snarled. "He sings that to everybody. I paid him to come here, girl. You hear what I'm saying? I paid him to come here and sing—just like I paid the dudes putting the food on the tables over there."

Jaris rolled his eyes. He whispered to Sereeta, "I hope this doesn't turn into a brawl. Marko's getting testy."

"If there's a food fight, there'll be plenty to throw around," Sereeta noted. "They're bringing in more trays."

Derrick and Destini wandered over. Derrick was grinning. He had that special look on his face that usually preceded his saying something dreadfully obtuse. He looked at Jasmine and remarked, "That dude was singing you a love song, Jasmine. I bet you were plenty jealous, huh Marko?"

"It wasn't a love song, you moron," Marko snarled. "Zendon's a jerk who's paid to sing drippy songs to girls having a birthday. He wouldn't care if he had to sing it to a pit bull!"

Destini glared at Marko. "Don't you call Derrick a moron, you nasty freak!" she hissed at Marko. "Why did you ever invite us to this idiotic party? We don't want to be here. Hardly anybody wants to be here, stupid!"

Oliver was near enough to glide in between Marko and Destini, who were now cursing each other with choice phrases. Derrick looked on in shock. "Well," Oliver shouted loudly, "I can see the food's here. Let's all mosey over there and get something to eat."

Jasmine jerked her hand free of Marko's grasp. She walked over to where Zendon was preparing another set. The moment she came close, Zendon turned and gave her a huge smile. "I swear," he cooed, "if you aren't the hottest chick in the universe, Jaz. You're so beautiful my eyes can hardly take it!"

Jasmine melted before the compliments. Marko rarely showered her with such effusive praise.

Nor did Marko have those dreamy, mesmerizing dark eyes that Zendon had. Nor did he have the smile that dazzled Jasmine. Zendon knelt down on the stage and reached out to hold Jasmine's hand.

"You were wonderful, Zendon," Jasmine purred. "Thank you for singing that beautiful song for me. This's been the best night of my entire life, and that's because of you. You're so talented. Someday you'll be a big star. You'll top the charts and win Grammies, and everybody'll love you!"

The band started playing, and Zendon took his place on the stage.

Marko stood there looking stunned. Pure hatred poured into his eyes. Jaris saw him close his hands into fists and bang his fists against his thighs in rage.

"Oh brother!" Jaris whispered to Sereeta. "This isn't good."

As the other musicians in After the Crash continued to play, Zendon came off the stage and took both Jasmine's hands. They began to dance. The other guests cleared a place for them as they spun around and held each other.

"I can't look!" Jaris exclaimed.

CHAPTER SIX

Sami Archer edged close to Jaris and Sereeta. "Am I confused here or what? I thought this was a party for Jasmine's eighteenth birthday. But it's lookin' like an engagement party for Jaz and that dude from the band. What's comin' down here? I'm missing somethin', gang."

"He's coming on strong to Jasmine," Alonee answered. "I think that's what he did with Carissa—when her and Kevin split up. I guess that's Zendon."

A few other couples began to dance. Marko cut across the room like a madman. He grabbed Zendon's shoulders, spun him around, and shoved him away from Jasmine. Then Marko dragged Jasmine into his arms and tried to dance with her. But she wasn't having any of it. "Let go of me, fool!" Jasmine screamed, trying to wriggle out of Marko's arms. Jasmine and Marko grappled awkwardly in the middle of the room. They made a terrible sight to see.

"I think the food is ready now!" Oliver shouted again. "Let's all head to the table. Get it while it's fresh."

Jaris added his strong baritone voice, "Real good food here. Yep. Good food. Come on! Let's eat."

Marko and Jasmine were in a standoff in the middle of the room. "I paid for all this, babe!" he shouted. "What you doin' to me, girl? You makin' a fool outta me, you know that? I paid for all this. For that idiot singer who's carryin' on like a lovesick donkey!"

"Nobody makin' a fool of you, Marko Lane," Jasmine shot back. "You doin' that all by your own self. And you doin' a great job, just like you always do. Zendon, he's a gentleman, which is something you know nothin' about, dude. You so jealous, you can't stand someone bein' nice to me. What's your problem, boy? Zendon, he's gonna be a big star pretty soon, and he likes me!"

"He's an idiot!" Marko screamed. "He's not gonna be no big star. He's a little creep who lives over on Grant with all the gang-bangers and the graffiti. He's trash, girl. He's garbage!"

"He's not trash!" Jasmine screamed back. "You the one who's trash. You're a trash-talkin' fool. I don't know why I bother with you. You're ruinin' my whole birthday party, dude, you know that? Look at everybody lookin' over at us and laughin'. We're like a sideshow in the circus. Marko, you're just ruinin' everything for me—and on my birthday!" Jasmine's voice dissolved into great sobs.

"I paid for all this!" Marko shouted. "My dad, he give me the money, and we paid for everything. Look how you're treating me, baby. You are breaking my heart. I done nothin' but good for you. And the first piece of garbage come along mouthin' lyin' sweet talk, you're sittin' on his lap, and I'm history. How you think that makes me feel?"

Sami shouted. "Come on, you two, quit your scrappin' and get some of this good eats. Food lookin' mighty good. Mmm-mmm, looka them little sandwiches! Don't they look good? They got liverwurst on them, looks like. I think maybe they call them canapés or somethin'. Ain't that what they call 'em, Matson?"

Matson Malloy stood at Sami's side with fear on his face. He had thought for a long time that Marko Lane was a monster. When they ran together on the Tubman track team, Marko had bullied and abused him. Everything happening at this party confirmed Matson's suspicion. Nothing good could come from anything connected with Marko. "Yeah, Sami. Canapés, I guess," Matson muttered.

Jaris and Sereeta were filling their paper plates with whatever they could quickly grab. "Sereeta," Jaris whispered, "remind me that, in the future, I must listen more to my pop. He told me not to come to this nightmare, but Mom made me come. Pop is *always* right. I must remember that."

"This canapé is very good," Sereeta declared.

"Hey, Matson," Marko called out. Of course, Marko was ignoring the fact that he had previously cruelly abused the shy, skinny youth. "You see what's goin' on, don't you? Man to man, I paid for all this for this chick's birthday party, and look how she's treatin' me?"

Matson concentrated on filling his plate with food. "You see her flirting with that trash up there, huggin' his stinkin' guitar," Marko ranted. "What a stinkin' freak he is. I pay him just to come and sing. Then he turns around and stabs me in the back by trying to steal my chick! He ain't even a good singer. He sounds like a dyin' cat with his whiny love songs to my chick—and puttin' his dirty hands on her. You seen that, right Matson?"

"No," Matson replied in a frightened voice. His plate was piled high, but Matson kept piling the food higher. He never looked up. "I think it happened when I went to the john. I think I gotta go again." Putting down his plate, he fled for the bathroom.

"Now you scared the poor boy off," Sami scolded. "Come on, Jaz, we're gonna cut the cake pretty soon and—"

"I don't . . . I don't feel like eating," Jasmine sobbed. "He's ruined everything." Jasmine began to sob loudly, attracting everyone's attention.

Zendon noticed Jasmine crying. Once again, he stepped off the stage and came toward her. "Hey, I don't want to see a pretty little thing like you crying on your birthday, sweetheart," Zendon cooed. He reached out for Jasmine with his graceful, long-fingered hands.

Marko leaped between Jasmine and Zendon. He yelled in Zendon's face. "Get back where you belong, you creep! Where you get off trying to steal my chick? What's the matter with you? Get back to your stinkin', trashy, gangbanger street. I see how you live over there. People throw their dirty mattresses in the alley, and the rats play tag all night. You're nothin' but ghetto!"

Zendon cast Marko a pitying smile. "I'm sorry, dude," he said in a steady voice. "But you're obviously a very sick dude. I'm not stealing your chick, man. You never had her." Zendon glanced around at the other partygoers now gathered in horrified little groups as limp balloons slowly sank to the floor. "Anybody here who can help this poor brother?" Zendon asked. "He's a sad case."

Jasmine's parents had agreed to stay away from the birthday party until all the guests had arrived and everything was in full swing. They planned to arrive when Jasmine opened her presents and then cut the cake. Then they'd go upstairs while the young people continued to party.

Things didn't turn out that way. As the Bensons pulled into the driveway, Zendon was running across the lawn toward his car, clutching his guitar. Marko was hurling clods of dirt taken from the newly sodded side lawn. One clod hit Zendon in the leg, causing him to run faster.

"What in—!" gasped Mrs. Benson.

Mr. Benson watched Zendon toss his guitar into the backseat and jump behind the wheel of the car. Marko heaved a parting shot of sod, hitting the windshield. The sod tumbled onto the hood, then dropped off as the car turned onto the street.

"Mom! Daddy!" Jasmine screamed, running toward her parents. "Marko . . . he . . . he . . . ruined everything. It was all so beautiful. The singer sang such a lovely birthday song to me, and I was so h-h-happy. Then Marko got jealous and ruined everything. Oh! I hate Marko Lane. I'll hate him forever and ever!"

Marko approached the Bensons. "She's lyin'," he screamed. "That freak Zendon

Corman, he came on to Jasmine. And she was goin' along with it like a trashy trick!"

Mr. Benson looked sternly at Marko. "Don't you call my daughter foul names, young man. I think it's best that you leave right now."

The other party guests began to leave, hurrying out the front door like people escaping a burning building. The other band members were packing up in a hurry too.

The Bensons took their sobbing daughter inside and upstairs. They spared everyone the awkward small talk that follows a party. Nobody had to thank the Bensons for offering their lovely home for the party. The Bensons didn't have to thank everybody for coming.

Jaris and Sereeta almost ran to Jaris's Honda. "Oh brother!" Jaris groaned. "I knew it'd be bad, but this was beyond my wildest nightmares."

"I was kinda surprised by that Zendon guy," Sereeta commented. "He was really flirting with Jasmine."

"You know how musicians are," Jaris replied. "They got big egos. They think they can make a girl's day by stuff like that. Marko should've just laughed it off."

On Monday morning at school, Marko didn't come swinging in with Jasmine as usual. He strode past the Harriet Tubman statue, his head down. Marko glanced at Jaris, but he didn't make any of his usual wisecracks. Jaris stared at him. Finally, Marko turned and snapped, "Whatcha gawking at, dude? Enjoyin' my misery?"

"No," Jaris answered.

"You got a big kick out of what happened at the party, didn't you, man?" Marko growled bitterly.

"No," Jaris responded. "It made me sick. I hated the whole thing."

Marko stood there, kicking at the dirt with his shoe. Finally he spoke. "She dumped me. Jasmine dumped me, man. After all I done for her too." Marko seemed devastated.

"She'll come around," Jaris consoled. "She's just pouting. You guys have had falling outs before, and she always comes back."

"Not this time," Marko declared. "She's gone crazy over that freak Zendon."

"Marko," Jaris advised, "last time you guys split up, Jasmine was crying her eyes out after a few days. Sami had to comfort her. She can't get along without you, brother."

"Last time we had trouble, she didn't have anybody else on the string," Marko replied. "This time she's got Zendon. I called her. I texted her. I tweeted. Nothin'. She won't even talk to me. I paid for that big party. It wasn't cheap, man. My dad footed the bill 'cause he knows how much Jasmine means to me.

Marko shook his head in disbelief. "I gave her a beautiful necklace for her birthday too. She didn't even mention it. I'm tellin' you, man, she's lost her mind over that Zendon. He's like cast an evil spell on the chick."

Jaris couldn't remember ever seeing Marko so upset. Jaris didn't like the guy, but he hated to see anybody so broken up.

"Marko," Jaris offered, "Carissa fell for that dude too, but she woke up quick. Now she's back with Kevin, and they're doing great. It'll be the same with Jaz. She'll get sick of him 'cause he's a phony. Zendon is one of those guys who goes from chick to chick like a hummingbird goes from flower to flower."

"You know what Jasmine's crazy mother told me?" Marko asked, his eyes wild. "She said Zendon asked Jasmine to sing for him. When she did, he said Jasmine has a great voice. Maybe she could be a vocalist in his stupid band. He said Jasmine has real talent. Jasmine can't sing worth nothin'. I've heard her, and she sounds like a howlin' cat."

Jaris couldn't say one way or the other. He'd never heard Jasmine sing.

"He's just lyin' to her," Marko ranted, "and she's dumb enough to believe it. He ain't never goin' to Vegas. He's gonna end up like the rest of them on Grant, lyin' on dirty mattresses in the alley and smoking dope. I think he's a doper right now. But now Jasmine's crazy mom is all excited too. She thinks her baby is gonna hitch herself to some risin' star like Zendon and his dumb band. The old lady is as crazy as Jasmine."

Jaris shook his head sadly. He hoped Jasmine would come back soon. Seeing Marko like this was almost worse than seeing him mean and cocky. He was like a brokenhearted madman.

When Jaris went off in another direction, Carissa approached him. She'd been standing nearby listening to part of the conversation between Marko and Jaris.

"I know what's happening to Jasmine," Carissa said. "Zendon can be so charming, so sweet. He made me feel like I was the most beautiful, most wonderful girl in the whole world. I really care for Kevin, but he's not very charming. I know he cares about me too. But he doesn't say all those magical things that Zendon does. Zendon's a player."

"My pop doesn't say charming things either to my mom," Jaris responded. "But I know he loves her more than his own life. You gotta watch these guys with a sugar line. They're like snake oil salesmen in the old days. They tell you what you want to hear."

Carissa's look said, "Tell me something I don't know."

"I love Sereeta with all my heart," Jaris went on. "I try to compliment her and stuff, but I'm not the kind of dude who can get all mushy. When I saw that Zendon crooning those stupid syrupy lyrics to Jasmine, I got sick to my stomach. If I started singing to Sereeta like that, she'd laugh out loud."

"Jaris," Carissa said after a long moment. "Zendon isn't a good guy."

Jaris looked hard at Carissa. He was puzzled. "What's that supposed to mean, Carissa?" he asked her.

"He's on crank, and he's done crack," Carissa explained. "When I caught him at it, he laughed. He said all musicians use junk, even the famous ones. He started listing names of people I've heard of, and he said they were junkies. I guess they were 'cause some of them are dead. He said I was stupid if I didn't realize that was part of the scene. He said it was okay . . . no problem."

"What a jerk!" Jaris exclaimed.

"He tried to get me to smoke some weed, but I wouldn't," Carissa continued. "That's sort of when I split from him. I got a little scared. I thought those dark eyes of his were so romantic. Then I really looked at him one night, and he looked scary. He looked *evil*."

Jaris wondered whether he should tell Marko what Carissa had just told him. He feared that Marko would get even crazier, so he decided against it. But what if Zendon was as bad as Carissa said? Jasmine was in a real bad place if she had become his girlfriend.

Before going to lunch with the gang under the eucalyptus trees, Jaris hung around the class where Jasmine was taking European history. She came out with the other students, but she was walking alone. Zendon wasn't in the class.

"You got a minute, Jaz?" Jaris called.

Jasmine shrugged. "Sure, Jare. Hey, man I'm sorry about what that fool Marko did at my party," Jasmine apologized. "It embarrassed me, and he made it miserable for everybody. My parents really freaked when I told them all what Marko did. I'm so done with Marko. Only good thing to come out of the whole mess, I got together with Zendon. He's so sweet and intelligent. I'm tellin' you, Jaris, I don't know why I stayed with that fool Marko for so long. Especially when there are guys like Zendon on campus. I been wasting my time with that moron, Marko."

Jasmine flashed her beautiful smile. "Zendon, he's got major talent," she went on. "And he even said maybe I could take voice lessons and sing with his band too when he hits the big time. Wouldn't that be amazing if I could ride to the top with him? He said I remind him of clips he's seen of a very young Whitney Houston. Wow, did that give me goose bumps. Uh . . . Jaris, what is it you wanted to talk about? I been rattlin' on." Jasmine giggled. She was in a happy mood.

"Jaz, lissen up," Jaris began. "I've had my problems with Marko too, you know that. Coupla times I wanted to strangle him. But this guy Zendon is no good for you, girl. I mean it."

"Where you come off sayin' that, Jaris?" Jasmine demanded, her eyes filling with anger.

"Somebody told me he's on crank," Jaris explained.

"Somebody is a big liar, boy," Jasmine snapped. "Zendon don't do no drugs, no way no how. He wouldn't touch them. I know a druggie when I see one, and he's clean. He's a good person, Jaris. He's the best thing ever happened to me. He's got a little place over on Grant, a garage like soundproofed and everything. He's doing a demo disc. He's this close"—Jasmine held her thumb and forefinger slightly apart— "to pullin' off a big deal. He says I can come over on weekends, and he'll teach me the guitar and stuff. I can practice with the band. I never in a million years thought something so exciting would happen to me."

"Jasmine, you just gotta be careful," Jaris urged, "y'hear what I'm sayin'? I don't know from my own eyes what Zendon is like. Someone I know to be an honest person told me he's doing drugs, and he's dangerous. Jaz, we've known each other for a long time. Yeah, we've never been friends. But I don't want something bad happenin' to you, girl, y'hear?"

For a long moment, Jasmine stared at Jaris. "Jaris, it touches my heart that you would care that much what happens to me. I guess I've made some mistakes. I haven't always been nice and everything, but I do respect you, Jaris."

Jasmine was speaking softly. "But you don't have to worry about me and Zendon. Zendon makes Marko look like spoiled cheese. Zendon is the real deal. Don't worry about this chick, Jaris. She just lucked into a beautiful new world, and she's flying high."

"Jaz, like I said," Jaris persisted, "I've had plenty problems with Marko. Ninety percent of the time, he's a jerk. He's been cruel and awful, and he's hurt people I love, like Sereeta. But Jaz, the guy does love you. Marko loves you. You should see him moping around like his life is over. He cares about you a lot. Don't take that lightly, girl."

"If he loved me," Jasmine countered, "he couldn't have done what he did the other night. He made a fool out of me and ruined my big night. I was looking forward to that party for a good long time, and he blew it for me."

"The sad thing is, Jasmine," Jaris insisted, "that he did all that stupid stuff because he does love you. He was crazy afraid that Zendon was stealing you away from him."

"I don't want that kind of love, Jaris," Jasmine stated. "I'm done with him. I got a dude now who respects and appreciates me. Zendon is awesome. I'm tellin' you, Jaris, once you get to know him better, you'll see what I'm sayin'. This is the best thing ever happened to me."

"Okay, Jasmine," Jaris relented. "I've had my say. I have the obligation to warn you about the stuff I heard. I want you to just remember this. As stupid and nasty as Marko Lane is, *he would never hurt you.*"

Jasmine stared wide-eyed at Jaris. "And you're sayin' Zendon might?" she demanded.

"I'm sayin' you don't know, girl. That's all I'm sayin'." Jaris left it at that.

CHAPTER SEVEN

Look Inessa," Chelsea cried as they rode their bikes to school. "There's a van and a pickup truck at the ghoul house. I wonder what happened?"

"Maybe that weird old couple got scared when you guys gave them that food. Maybe they took off. Now somebody's cleaning up the dump," Inessa noted. "I'm glad. Them being there made me feel funny."

"There's Shadrach!" Chelsea pointed.

"I don't want nothing to do with him," Inessa declared, screwing up her face. "I don't care what anybody says. He's weird."

"Hi, Shadrach," Chelsea yelled, pulling her bike into the driveway of the ghoul house. "What's hap'nin'?"

Shadrach smiled and answered. "It all started when you wanted to help these folks, girl, you and your friends. I talked to Pastor Bromley. I told the people at the church how these folks're livin' in an abandoned house. They had no running water, no electricity. So we found a retired couple having trouble making their own mortgage, and they got room for them. These folks can kick in a little rent money, and that'll help everybody. Chelsea, none of this would have happened if you guys hadn't taken an interest and raised money for the food basket."

"Wow!" Chelsea exclaimed. "See Inessa?"

Pastor Bromley appeared then, pushing the lady in the wheelchair. She looked confused, but she was smiling. Her husband walked alongside her. "Be just fine, Lavinia," he said soothingly. "Gonna be just fine now. These folks are gettin' a decent place for us to live."

Inessa hung back, looking annoyed. Chelsea shook hands with the old couple.

The old man spoke to her. "We from Alabama, and we raised five children there. But Lavinia's arthritis actin' up, and we came west to here. For a while, I worked, and we was okay. But now I got the arthritis too. You must be one of the young 'uns who gave help to us—the oranges and the tuna. Good Lord bless ya! Sun beginnin' to shine on us. Yessirree!"

"I'm happy for you," Chelsea responded, delighted by how it all turned out.

Inessa yelled from the sidewalk. "Come *on*! We'll be late for school!"

"I'm coming," Chelsea shouted, waving to Shadrach as she joined Inessa. "Inessa, everything is working out good!"

"I don't know," Inessa complained. "My parents always say that when people are poor, it's mostly their own fault. They didn't work hard enough, or they didn't save their money like they should. Those old people were probably lazy when they were young. Otherwise, they'd have something put away for their old age. Maybe they drank liquor or gambled or did bad things like that."

Chelsea liked Inessa, but she wasn't a really close friend. She wasn't as close to Chelsea as Athena and Keisha were. Chelsea thought Inessa was kind of selfish and hard-hearted. Chelsea had only lived fourteen or so years so far. But she'd already seen a lot of good hardworking people beaten down by bad luck, illness, or other misfortune.

Chelsea thought of the man down the street who ran a grocery store. He charged outrageous prices for low-quality food, just because he could. A lot of his customers were poor people without cars. They couldn't get to the bigger stores where things were cheaper and of better quality. That grocer was getting rich by being a cheat. Many of his customers were suffering through no fault of their own. Chelsea saw many examples of life not being fair. She felt sorry for people in trouble.

Jaris Spain was now assistant manager of the Chicken Shack where he worked. He'd been given a nice increase in salary, which he appreciated. His old Honda was having increasing problems, and he hoped to get a better used car. To save the sputtering Honda for as long as he could, Jaris now usually jogged or rode his old motorcycle to work.

That night, he rode his motorcycle home at about ten-fifteen. He noticed a group of boys milling around the street just ahead. He'd seen Nite Ryders around here before, and a shiver of fear ran up his spine. Not long ago, back when he was a junior, he ran into Shane Burgess on this stretch of road. Shane was tagging that night, marking turf.

As Jaris got closer, he recognized some of the boys as Tubman dropouts. These kids all had the same dismal story. They were losing their way. First they dropped out of school. Then they joined a gang.

Jaris saw Shane Burgess standing alongside Brandon Yates. Brandon had been a troublemaker from way back. He tried to date Chelsea, and Jaris had to run him off.

Jaris slowed on the motorcycle, calling out, "Hey Shane! How's it goin', man?"

Only Shane and Brandon were left in the faint glow of a nearby streetlight. The other boys had melted into the darkness. Shane looked awful. He had been a good-looking kid, but now he looked wasted. If you didn't know him, you'd think he was over thirty instead of just a teenager. Dark circles hung below his eyes, and he looked gaunt. He was probably doing so much dope that he wasn't eating regularly.

Brandon looked bad too. He'd spent time in drug rehab. From the looks of him, the treatment hadn't done him much good.

Shane didn't say anything. He knew how much the kids at Tubman High loved and respected his sister. They all knew what she was trying to do for him. After he first moved in with Ms. McDowell in her condo, he began to look clean and healthy. Now he looked dirty, guilty, and defiant, all at the same time. He was sullen. He didn't have to say he no longer lived with his sister. Jaris knew it.

"You're Nite Ryders now, right?" Jaris asked both Shane and Brandon.

"You said it, man!" Brandon snapped. He was always a punk. At least he struck Jaris that way. Jaris had some serious run-ins with him to protect Chelsea from his bad influence.

"Know anything about what went down the other night on Grant?" Jaris asked the two boys. "That dude from Lincoln getting capped."

"You The Man or what?" Brandon growled. "Where you get off questioning us, Spain?" When Jaris first met Brandon, he was wild, but he had enough sense to be scared. Now he looked as hard as the granite in the nearby hills.

"I'm just wondering," Jaris answered. "Shane, don't you mind hurting your sister like this? Doesn't that bother you, man?"

Shane didn't say anything. He looked down at the ground.

"The other night after the murder on Grant," Jaris went on, "me and my friends almost got killed. A dark sedan was hauling it from the crime scene. It nearly hit us head-on. We figured the dudes in that car were running away from Grant. We figured they just got done shooting that kid from Lincoln . . ."

When Shane's head came up, there was pure terror on his face. Brandon looked ill at ease too. Jaris had struck a nerve. He got a sinking feeling in the pit of his stomach. These two were in that car all right. Jaris thought it was Shane at the wheel. Now he was sure.

"Lotta guys took off when that happened," Brandon remarked in a shaky voice. "Nobody wants to be around when the ghetto birds show up. Y'hear what I'm sayin'? The place was crawlin' with cops. Cops came around later too. Cops in dark suits digging for clues. But over on Grant they don't rat out brothers."

"We don' know nothin' about what happened on Grant," Shane declared. "Whatever the fight was, we didn' have no dog in it. We had no score with the dude from Lincoln."

"Shane, you need to get clean, man," Jaris advised. "You need to go into rehab and salvage yourself, dude."

Brandon laughed bitterly. "Rehab's a crock, man."

Jaris ignored Brandon and spoke directly to Shane. "You know what you're doing to your sister, Shane? She went out on a limb for you. She loves you, man. You think she deserves what you're putting her through? You're breaking her heart, Shane. You wanna be doing that?"

"Let's split, man," Brandon urged. "We don' need to lissen to this dude."

Shane waited a moment longer, then he looked Jaris right in the eye. "We didn' do nothin'. We didn' kill nobody. I never killed nobody. I tried change things with my sister. I tried, but I couldn't walk the line, man. I walk crooked, and the line she put down was too straight. She needs to forget about me."

The two boys then joined the others in the darkness. Jaris wasn't sure how he felt. He didn't think Brandon and Shane had killed Buster Bennett, but he wasn't sure. They were both into drugs. They might have been high enough that night to do anything. One thing Jaris knew for sure: Ms. McDowell could never forget Shane.

At Tubman High the next day, Marko Lane was a picture of despair. Even his usual crowd abandoned him because he was no fun anymore. He spent all his time moaning over the loss of Jasmine Benson and cursing Zendon.

"That boy turnin' into a head case," Sami Archer declared. "I feel bad for him, even though he never very likable—to say the least."

Marko went to his classes like a zombie. He didn't participate in the discussion. Everybody saw not the wisecracking, laughing face, but a stranger. Marko was a glum, blank-eyed ghost of his former self.

Later in the day, Sami approached Marko. "Dude, me and Matson goin' to a movie tonight. Why don't you ask Neely Pelham to go? We'll all go together. She got the hots for you, Marko. Anybody can see that."

Marko was staring at Sami as if he didn't know her. "She been eyeballin' you," Sami went on, "ever since the word got out about you and Jaz. She'd grab your arm in a minute, boy. I ain't made sense of it yet, but you can turn on most chicks, Marko. What you say? The four of us could have some fun. You could get your mind off that wandering chick of yours."

Marko answered in a whine. "I don't want nobody else but Jasmine. I don't know why she's doing this to me. I been so good to her. I've given her really expensive gifts and taken her to nice places. It's like Zendon put a spell on her. I wish Zendon would drop dead."

"Don't you be talkin' like that, boy," Sami commanded. "Lissen up. You gotta pull yourself together. You gonna be a nervous wreck. When she finally comes back, you won't even be able to handle it."

"After school," Marko replied, "Zendon's taking Jasmine over to that sound studio to practice with his band. He's got her head turned around backwards. She thinks she'll be like that Rihanna or something"

"Boy, you start hangin' with Neely, and Jasmine gonna get jealous," Sami advised. "You gotta fight fire with fire, Marko. Jasmine gonna think , 'Hey look! Old Marko ain't missin' me. He got a new chick. Maybe I better rethink this whole deal.'"

"You know what?" Marko responded darkly. "When that dude from Lincoln got capped on Grant—you know, Zendon's cousin—Zendon was standin' right there. Shots were flyin' all over the place. Too bad Zendon didn't get capped instead of that other guy. It said in the paper that this Buster dude was a good guy. Why did he have to die and a devil like Zendon get to live. You answer me that, Sami?"

Just then, Jasmine and Zendon were walking across the Tubman campus, arm in arm. Jasmine kept looking up at Zendon, giggling.

"Look at her!" Marko remarked bitterly. "She's turned into a complete fool. Look at that chick. She ain't got a brain cell left in her head."

Marko walked toward the pair. In his heart, he knew Sami was right. He should be making up to Neely or some other cute babe. That would have gotten Jasmine's attention more than his anger. But he was hurting too much to make sensible decisions. All he wanted to do was to somehow get rid of Zendon and get his girl back. That's all he could think of, day and night.

"Hey, Jasmine!" Marko called out to her. "You like that necklace I gave you for your birthday? I told my dad we needed to get the best for you. We spent a lot of money on that necklace. You didn't even say nothin' about it. How come you didn't even thank me, girl? You got no feelings for me no more after all we been through together. We been hangin' together a long time, girl."

"I'll give you the old necklace back if you want," Jasmine retorted. She looked at Zendon and remarked, "He doesn't know how to take no for an answer. He thinks he's such hot stuff that no girl in her right mind would choose somebody else over him."

Zendon threw back his head and laughed. Marko wanted to punch him in the face. He wanted to see all his pretty, shiny teeth scattered on the walkway. Marko wished with all his heart that Zendon would die.

"Jasmine," Marko told her, "this dude don't care about you. You just a hot chick on his arm this week. Pretty soon he gets tired of you and finds somebody else. He's gonna toss you in the dump, girl, y'hear me?"

Jaris and Sereeta walked past the yelling match between Marko and Jasmine.

"You're just making it worse," Jaris remarked to Marko.

Marko took time out to snap at Jaris. "What do you know about the pain I'm feelin', man?" Marko shot back. "What if that Zendon lured Sereeta away like he did Jaz. I'd like to see you then, dude. You'd be worse than me."

Marko's head swung back in Jasmine's direction. "You just making a big fool of yourself like you always do, Marko," she yelled. "Ever since I known you, you been makin' a show of yourself. You always makin' me look bad too 'cause I was with you. Well, I ain't with you no more."

Jaris had noticed Marko's hands swinging at his sides. Win or lose, having a fistfight with Zendon was a bad idea. Zendon was a little more muscular and beefier than Marko. And he was probably stronger. But Marko was a good athlete. He had a lot of strength. If Marko decided to take Zendon on, Marko figured he'd get the worst of it. And he'd be kicked out of Tubman for fighting. Fighting was strictly against the rules. And what would it accomplish anyway? If, improbably, Marko won the fight and left Zendon beaten up in the dust, Jasmine would only run over to him and care for him. She would only curse Marko for his brutality. If, as was more likely, Zendon beat Marko, Jasmine would probably laugh and call Marko a pathetic weakling.

Marko couldn't win.

Over on Grant, police investigators were going through the neighborhood.

They were talking to whoever was willing to talk to them. The willing witnesses were few in number. But the police were getting some valuable anonymous tips.

On Monday, two police investigators came to Torie McDowell's home. They wanted to talk to Shane Burgess. He was no longer living at Ms. McDowell's condo, but she had his cell phone number. She called Shane and told him to come to the condo because the police had questions for him.

Shane arrived in less than an hour.

"We'd like to know where you were on the night of the murder, Shane," one investigator asked him.

"Me and my homies were drivin' around," Shane answered. "We were just hangin'."

They had a string of other questions. Did Shane have any evidence that he wasn't on Grant Street that night? What were the names and addresses of his "homies?"

Eventually, they told Shane that they had a lot of tips about a dark sedan fleeing the scene right after the shooting. They asked him about his car. Shane went outside with them to look at his fifteen-year-old dark Chevrolet sedan. It was parked alongside his sister's Honda Accord.

The investigators checked out the car, maybe for new dents or scrapes. They asked to look inside. Shane just shrugged. Ms. McDowell prayed they wouldn't find anything incriminating, like drugs or weapons.

They found nothing. The older of the two investigators told Shane they would be talking to him again soon. They emphasized the word "soon." Then they thanked Shane and Ms. McDowell, and they left.

When they were gone, Ms. McDowell swung around to face her brother.

"You're with the Nite Ryders again. Aren't you, Shane?" Ms. McDowell asked sadly. "A lot of kids from Tubman see you tagging and doing drugs around the neighborhood. I can see by looking at you, Shane. You're in trouble."

"That's all lies," Shane protested. "I just hang with some of the guys I used to know. I don't do drugs, Torie."

"Oh Shane, you were doing so well. I was so hopeful," Ms. McDowell sighed. "Then everything began to change."

"Listen, I'm fine," Shane assured her. "I just can' take school. I'm workin' now, just odd jobs, but I'm makin' out okay. I'm not a big brain like you. School ain't workin' for me. I gotta do it my own way."

"You're with Brandon Yates a lot," his sister accused him. "I'm hearing that. He dropped out of Tubman and went to rehab, but it didn't help. He's just going to drag you down, Shane."

Ms. McDowell's eyes were filled with worry. She was close to tears. "Shane," she said to him softly, "when you were born, I was thirteen years old. I remember the beautiful big-eyed baby that you were. I fell in love with my baby brother. I wasn't old enough to help you then, Shane, to keep you out of the foster homes, all that stuff.

We were all on a sinking ship—you and me, our parents, our siblings."

Painful memories filled her mind. "I couldn't save you then," she continued. "I could hardly save myself. But you and me, we're all that's left of our family, honey. I love you so much. I'd do anything to get you back on the right track. Just tell me what you need, Shane."

"I'm okay, Torie," Shane insisted. "I'm okay, honest. I'm not doin' anything bad. I'm just hangin' with my friends and gettin' a lot of stuff out of my system. I'll go back to school sooner or later. I'll be fine."

"I hate to think of you out at night, hanging on those mean streets, Shane," Ms. McDowell sighed. "When those police officers showed up, I almost died. You were around there when that boy was killed. I know you were. The night it happened I couldn't sleep. I thought you were in the middle of it somehow. I tortured myself with worry. And now the policemen come here and I'm not sure if . . ." She couldn't finish her sentence.

"They got nothin'," Shane declared. "They're lookin' under rocks. They're harassing all the young guys. You know how they do it. Me and my homies were drivin' around, yeah. But we weren't anywhere near where that dude was shot. I mean, look, the cops are knocking on everybody's door."

"Do you think the police investigators went to the Spain house and asked about their son?" Ms. McDowell asked in her best teacher's voice. "Do you think they went to the Shaw house? I doubt the police went to the houses of any of my students, Shane. They came here because they were suspicious of what you might be involved in. You're in with the Nite Ryders. They do drugs. They do violence. Even if you're not a Nite Ryder, just being with them makes you look bad."

The sister paused for a moment and then asked, "Shane, where are you living?"

"Me and some guys just hangin' at an apartment," the boy answered. "We all chip in for the rent."

"Shane, you have a nice bedroom here," Ms. McDowell commented. "I haven't changed anything in your room since you left. Please come home, Shane. It's no good for you to hang at some apartment. Those guys're just going to get you in deeper."

Shane looked up over his sister's head with an expression of desperation. He couldn't look her in the eyes. "I can't come back here. It stifles me," he responded.

"Please Shane, I'm begging you," Ms. McDowell pleaded. "Come home. Go back to school." She was trembling.

Shane looked at his sister. He loved her. He knew she loved him. He didn't want to cause her pain. But he couldn't come back either. It was too late for him to change now. He wanted to be with his friends. He wanted to do drugs as they did. His sister would try to stop him.

"I'm sorry, Torie," Shane replied, heading for his car. "I'll . . . uh . . . keep in touch, okay?" He got behind the wheel of his car, closed the door, and drove away slowly.

CHAPTER EIGHT

Chelsea didn't spend a lot of time with Sharon, her friend over on Grant. Chelsea liked Sharon a lot. But Mom didn't allow Chelsea to spend any time in that neighborhood. The only time the girls got together was at Tubman or when somebody dropped Sharon off at the Spain house.

That afternoon, one of Sharon's cousins dropped her at Chelsea's house. Then the girls took the bus to the mall. Now that Chelsea wasn't grounded anymore, she could take the bus. Jaris didn't have to drive her.

Neither girl had much money to spend, but it was fun going into the stores. Then they'd stop at the food court for snacks and icy drinks. Chelsea had enough money to buy a top if it was on sale. Sharon's mother was a single mom on a tight budget. Sharon had just enough to buy some cheap fashion jewelry.

"You got a boyfriend, Chelsea?" Sharon asked as they drank an icy strawberry drink.

"No," Chelsea responded. "Maurice Moore says stupid things to me. So I guess he likes me, but I don't like him. Heston Crawford is okay, but he's kind of a nerd. I think I like Heston, but Pop says I'm too young for a boyfriend."

"We're almost fifteen," Sharon asserted. "Some of my cousins got babies already, and they're not much older."

"I wouldn't like that," Chelsea declared. "*You* got a boyfriend, Sharon?"

"Uh-huh. His name is Keone Lowe," Sharon answered. "He's nice. Sometimes we just sit out on the curb and talk. But Mama won't let me do that no more 'cause of the shooting."

"If I told Pop I had a boyfriend," Chelsea confided, "he'd like freak. He calls me 'little girl' all the time. I think he sees me as somebody eleven or something. Sharon, are you scared? Do you think the guys who killed that Lincoln boy are going to come back and hurt somebody else?"

Sharon shrugged. "Guys always speeding around at night, yelling at other guys. Fights break out. They hang out the car windows and diss each other. Sometimes they shoot. Goes on all the time. Tubman boys hate Lincoln boys, and the Links hate Tubman guys. They jump each other for no reason sometime."

"You think that's what happened with the Bennett guy? That a Tubman guy hit him just 'cause he went to Lincoln?" Chelsea asked.

"I don't know," Sharon replied. "Maybe. Lotsa guys on Grant don't go to any school no more. Girls too. They drop out. I hate living over there on Grant, Chelsea, but Mom can't afford no place better. It's the Nite Ryders' hood."

Sharon sipped her drink through the straw. "Nobody on our street ever seems to get nowhere," she continued, "except maybe that Zendon Corman. He says he's gonna be rich and famous 'cause of that band he's got. He calls it After the Crash, but I don't like it. I don't like Zendon either. He's kinda mean sometimes."

"Know what?" Chelsea said. "Zendon came to this girl Jasmine Benson's birthday party. He sang to her and stuff. But Jasmine had a boyfriend there. Now he's real mad 'cause Zendon stole her away from him. It got real ugly. My brother went to the party. Jasmine and her boyfriend were yelling and screaming. My brother said it was the worst party he ever went to. Jaris doesn't like Zendon either."

"Zendon got a lotsa girlfriends," Sharon remarked, "'cause he's handsome. All his girlfriends are pretty. He's got this little garage where he practices. Sometimes he takes the girls there, and they sing with the band. He tells 'em all that they got good voices and maybe could be like Beyoncé or Rihanna."

Sharon giggled. "But it's all lies," she went on. "My mom doesn't have anything to do with the Cormans. Mama doesn't have many friends on Grant. She says most of them are in trouble, and she wants no part of them. I think they do crank. I wish we could move, Chelsea."

"I wish you could too," Chelsea said.

The girls finished their icy drinks and headed for a clothing store that catered to teenagers. Music was blasting away, and Chelsea laughed. "When I was grounded, poor Jaris had to come shopping with me. He just hated this store, Sharon."

Sharon found a pretty green necklace for under two dollars. "This is gonna look so good with this green top I got, Chelsea," she commented.

Chelsea was checking out the sales rack where tops were displayed. "I could afford one of these," Chelsea noted.

"Look at the destroyed denim, Chelsea," Sharon pointed. "And look at the crops. Ohhh, but they're so expensive!

"Look, isn't this a cute cami?" Chelsea noted. "You buy one and you get one free!"

The girls rushed to the fitting room so that Chelsea could try on several tops.

Sharon watched Chelsea slip into a blue cami. "Ohhh, you're so pretty, Chelsea," Sharon told her.

"Thanks," Chelsea said. "You are too."

"No, I'm not," Sharon protested. "My nose is too big, and I got zits."

"Your nose is cute, and the zits'll go away," Chelsea declared, turning around and around to check out the cami.

"I bet I'll always be stuck in places like Grant," Sharon commented. "Sometimes Mama gets real depressed, and she says people like us never get nowhere. We're losers. One day the same as the one before. Mama drinks beer when she's depressed. I don't like that. She's not like my mama when she drinks. She gets mean and hollers at me. She tells me I got to stop looking at boys altogether 'cause that's what got her life ruined. She says Keone Lowe is a bum, just like my daddy was. I need to stop sitting on the curb with him."

Sharon held up one of the camis that Chelsea was trying on. "But when Mama don't drink," she continued, "she's really nice, Chelsea." Sharon turned wistful. "I bet that old Zendon will get his dream. He'll probably be rich and famous like some big idol. He come over one day. He started in talking to some boys hangin' 'round the building. Zendon was bragging up a storm. He says he's already got a lotta money. He needs to buy expensive instruments so his band sounds good. He said he's gonna get good gigs and make tons of money. Then he's gonna take Las Vegas by storm."

"Maybe," Chelsea asserted. "But my brother says Zendon isn't that good. He was crooning some dopey song to Jasmine

Benson. He sounded like some boring old singer that my grandmother used to listen to. His song had no beat or anything."

"The brothers," Sharon responded, "they told Zendon that nobody gets out of Grant. The only way is if the undertaker or the cops take them out. Everybody stuck here, they say. Zendon got mad. He said he's getting out, and nobody ever gonna stop him. The dudes just laughed. They say Zendon was talking smack. Zendon's dreams gonna go bust just like all the other dreams on Grant."

Chelsea picked a cami to buy, and the two girls left the fitting room. Chelsea was buying the blue one and getting the yellow one free.

"Where does Zendon get the money to buy all his good instruments, Sharon?" Chelsea wondered. "He have a job or something? I don't think they pay him much for those gigs around the neighborhood."

At the checkout counter, Sharon paid for her green necklace. "I don't know. But he's always got a fat wallet, stuffed with money."

"You think he's dealing, Sharon?" Chelsea asked as she paid for her cami.

Sharon's eyes got very big. "They're buying and selling all the time on Grant," the girl declared. "Mama says, when it comes to dealin', we gotta be like those three monkeys you see all the time. You know how one's coverin' his eyes, and one his ears, and one his mouth. It says, 'See no evil, hear no evil, speak no evil.'"

Sharon was speaking more loudly and faster than usual. "Mama says dealin' is way different than a shootin'. She says, with the dealers, we don't see nothin', we don't hear nothin', and we don't say nothin'. We do, and we'll just get dead like Buster Bennett."

Chelsea and Sharon took the trolley and then the bus home. Chelsea's new cami had a plunging neckline. She was thinking how she could get it past Pop. She had a little fringe vest, she remembered, that she could

wear over the cami. Then Pop wouldn't no-
tice the neckline. When Chelsea got to
school, she could take the vest off.

Sharon got off the bus first. Chelsea
waved to her as she started toward Grant.
Chelsea felt sorry for Sharon. She hoped
she wouldn't be stuck on Grant forever as
her mom said.

It was almost dark when Chelsea
walked up her own driveway. Then she saw
Grandma Jessie's little red sports car parked
there. Chelsea hated to see Grandma Jessie.
She always brought trouble. Last time she
came, she tried to get Chelsea sent away to
some ritzy boarding school up north. Then
she tried to talk Mom out of signing the
mortgage on the house so that Pop could
buy his own garage—Spain's Auto Care.
Having his own business meant the world to
Pop.

"Hello, Chelsea," Grandma Jessie
greeted her sweetly. "My goodness, you are
getting more lovely each day. Did you buy
something nice at the mall? I see from your

bag that you've been to—what's the name of that place? I can't read it—the name on that strange little purple bag."

"It's called Dark Angst," Chelsea replied.

"Oh dear!" Grandma Jessie remarked. "I hope it's not a witchcraft store."

"They have spooky stuff like skeletons and skulls on the clothes," Chelsea responded. "But they have nice stuff too. I got this nice cami." She lifted it from the bag and waved it in the air.

"Sweet," Grandma Jessie commented. "Your mother and I were talking. A nice new housing development is going in across town. The prices are just so amazing, considering the amenities. Not like . . . this . . . house."

A shudder seized Grandma's body. She glanced up at the popcorn ceiling. "Honestly Monica, I just cannot believe you still have a popcorn ceiling. I mean, every single person I know has gotten that ugly old stuff removed. Now they have lovely modern

157

smooth ceilings. I mean, honestly, the popcorn ceilings are so done with!"

"I always sorta liked the popcorn ceiling," Chelsea remarked. "Remember Pop saying how good it is 'cause it doesn't show the dirt?" As soon as Chelsea made the comment, she regretted it. It made Pop sound like just what Grandma Jessie thought he was. To Grandma, Pop was a coarse, crude cave dweller who appreciated a ceiling because it hid the filth of years of dwelling in this house.

"We just never got around to removing the popcorn, Mom," Mom said. "Maybe this year." The truth was that nobody in the Spain family was the least bit bothered by the old popcorn ceiling.

Grandma Jessie cast another disgusted look at the ceiling. "It's just so . . . so out-of-date. I think I even see several spider's webs over in the corner. I suppose the spiders are pleased enough by the rough surface. It makes it easier for them to cling to the ceiling."

Chelsea heard Jaris arrive on his motorcycle. She could imagine what he was thinking at the sight of the little red convertible. She had thought the same thing. Until now it had been a pretty good day, but all that was about to change.

"Anyway," Grandma Jessie continued, "this new development has grand kitchens with glorious granite counters and—"

Jaris came in. "Hi, Grandma," he greeted through gritted teeth.

"Hello, dear," Grandma chirped. "Did you just ride in on a motorcycle?"

"Uh yeah," Jaris replied. "Sometimes I use the motorcycle. Saves gas. Extends the life of my car too."

"Mmm," Grandma Jessie hummed. "I suppose you all must scrimp and scrape now. I mean, your father has put that huge new mortgage on the house to buy his pet garage. Anyway, when I hear motorcycles, I always think of those dreadful gangs."

"Yeah, well, I got an old chopper," Jaris responded. "Lotsa guys ride 'em. Nice, you know . . . regular guys." Jaris said. He glanced at Chelsea.

"Well, your mother and I have been talking about this marvelous new housing development across town—far from here," she began again. "When the housing bubble burst, prices just came down so much. You can get these beautiful homes—"

"We sorta like it here, Grandma," Jaris interrupted.

"Oh, Chelsea!" Grandma said, ignoring Jaris. "If you could see the bedrooms in these new houses. They are so lovely, especially for a young girl like you. Wonderful oval mirrors where the dressing table goes, and the color scheme—"

"I feel at home here," Chelsea asserted.

Pop's pickup came roaring into the driveway, completing the slowly unfolding disaster. He parked right next to the little red convertible. Grandma Jessie peered out the window, "He came in very close," she noted. "I do hope he didn't scrape the side of my car."

"We woulda heard the crash, Grandma," Jaris noted.

Pop flung open the door. "Hey! What a great surprise Monie! Your mom's come to visit!" he roared.

"Oh, we were just visiting, Lorenzo," Mom said nervously. "Mom is telling me about this nice new housing development across town."

"Oh, beautiful," Pop declared. "We're having the why-are-you-still-living-in-this-ratty-old-house discussion. A man prays he gets the chance to come home to this."

"I was just saying, Lorenzo," Grandma Jessie explained, "how do you stand that horrid popcorn ceiling? It is *decades* behind the times. How can you tolerate such ugly décor?"

"Oh, well, see it has got its advantages, Jessie," Pop responded. "See, we make a lot of popcorn. Sometimes the lid comes off the popper and some of this here popcorn goes flying up to the ceiling. There's lot of grime up there, so it sticks. That's okay, 'cause it adds more insulation. Looks okay too. See, if we got rid of the popcorn deal, then the nice smooth ceiling would have little clusters of popcorn stickin' up there. Now that wouldn't look so good."

"Very amusing, Lorenzo," Grandma Jessie remarked. "You should have been a comedian." She was starting to say something else when another car screeched into the driveway, parking right behind the little red convertible.

Jaris looked out the window to see Marko Lane getting out of his car. Marko hardly ever came to the Spain house. The last time was when Marko was thirteen. His mother made him come to apologize. Marko had "accidentally" thrown his skateboard through the Spain's front window. Jaris thought this was really an bad time for Marko to be making his first visit in four years.

Pop went to the door. "Hey, listen, is this here a red letter day or what?" he declared. "All my favorite people comin' to visit. We got Grandma Jessie here telling us how ugly our popcorn ceiling is. Now here's our buddy, Marko Lane, the bully of Tubman High School."

Marko barged in, ignoring the look of horror on the face of the older woman seated in the high-backed chair. "I got problems," Marko gasped. "Jaris, I just heard something. I gotta know if it's true or not."

"What's that, Marko?" Jaris asked.

Grandma Jessie had been sipping green tea, but now she spilled a little of it on her white blouse.

"Zendon, that freak who stole Jasmine from me," Marko blurted. "They're sayin' he's a crack dealer. He's the big drug dealer over on Grant!"

Grandma Jessie gasped. She sank back in her chair, looking at her daughter with a horrified expression.

"Well Marko, I heard that too," Jaris replied. "But I'm not sure. I told Jasmine to be careful, but she's not listening too good right now."

"Man, I gotta get her away from this dude, Jaris," Marko exclaimed. "He's a monster. I can't stand by while Jasmine gets in deeper with a criminal drug dealer. She could get killed." Marko was almost sobbing.

Grandma Jessie seemed about to swoon. She turned to her daughter. "Monica, who is this boy?" she asked in a whisper.

"Marko Lane. He goes to school with Jaris," Mom replied tersely.

"Jaris, my grandson, is in a nest of drug dealers?" Grandma Jessie moaned, clutching her chair. "Ohhh, it's worse that I thought."

"Marko," Jaris advised, "if you're sure of this, you need to talk to Jasmine's parents. That's the only way to get her out of there."

"Man, *I can't*," Marko cried. "They hate me, dude. They've always hated me. They never thought I was good enough for Jasmine. But since that party, they hate me even more. Jasmine told them all the fighting was my fault. If I show up at the front door of the Benson house, they'll probably call the cops on me."

Jaris sighed, "Tell you what, man, I always got along good with the Bensons. They're not my favorite kind of people. But they've always been polite to me and my folks. I'll go over there with you."

Grandma Jessie turned once more to her daughter and asked, "Jaris is going off with *him*?"

"He may have to," Mom replied. "We can't let Jasmine get into something where she could end up hurt—or worse."

"Can you come right away, Jaris?" Marko begged. He finally noticed Grandma Jessie then. "Hey old lady," he said, "I'm sorry if I upset you so much you spilled your beer on your blouse or something. But some criminal has got my chick, and I gotta save her."

"It is *not* beer, young man," Grandma Jessie croaked.

"Whatever!" Marko said. "Come on, Jaris. Hurry man!"

Jaris and Marko rushed out the door to Marko's car. Grandma Jessie closed her eyes and rocked back and forth in her chair. "It is so dreadful," she moaned. "It is all so dreadful. A rude youth barging in with horror stories of girls under the control of criminals. My grandson rushing away with this strange, wild young man. It's like another world, a dark and frightening world . . ."

CHAPTER NINE

"Who told you about Zendon being a drug dealer, Marko?" Jaris asked as they drove through the darkness.

"Tommy Jenkins," Marko replied, "Trevor's brother. He met a guy at the community college. The guy said Zendon is the go-to guy if you want crack or meth or anything. Tommy said he heard my chick was with Zendon. He wanted to give me a heads-up if I wanted to do something about it. Man, that's how that stinkin' dude gets all that fancy stuff for his band. That's where the sound system and all that stuff comes from. He's financing his stupid dead-end music career on crack, and he wants to take Jasmine down with him."

"I heard the same story too, from Carissa Polson," Jaris revealed. "Sounds like it's true, man."

Marko pulled into the Benson driveway, and both boys went to the door. Mr. Benson answered the ring. He didn't know Jaris well, but his gaze focused squarely on Marko. "You are not welcome at this house," he stated sharply. "How dare you come here? You caused my daughter such shame and embarrassment at her birthday party. You acted like a wild beast, Lane, and we shall never forget it."

"Mr. Benson," Jaris cut in, "I know all about that party, and you're right. Marko was off the wall. But we're here about something else, and it's really important. Marko is worried about Jasmine's safety with Zendon Corman."

Mr. Benson continued to glare at Marko. "I'm sure you care about my daughter's safety. After all, you reduced her to hysterics by your behavior, Lane."

"Mr. Benson, please listen," Jaris pleaded. "We believe Zendon Corman is a drug dealer, and Jasmine is at risk."

"What utter nonsense!" Mr. Benson cried, now looking scornfully at Jaris. "I thought you had a better character than this, Jaris. My wife and I have worked with your parents. We're all on committees at Marian Anderson Middle School and Tubman High. They are upstanding people."

Mr. Benson glowered at Jaris. "I am utterly shocked that you are helping Marko Lane. You are propagating a preposterous lie about young Zendon just so that Lane can get back into my daughter's life. I have a good mind to call your parents. I should tell them you are participating in Lane's evil scheme."

"Mr. Benson," Jaris persisted, "I understand how you feel—"

"Poor Jasmine!" Mr. Benson cut him off. "She was so upset after that farce of a party. My wife and I took hours to try to calm her down. Zendon was very helpful in comforting Jasmine as well. He is a perfect gentleman—unlike you, Lane. My daughter has finally come to her senses about her ill-fated relationship with you, Lane."

Mr. Benson glared at each boy in turn. "I warn you, Marko Lane," the man declared, "do not come here again. Jaris, you'd better rethink helping this punk in his evil scheming."

"Mr. Benson," Jaris said desperately. "Could we talk to your wife? We have solid information that Zendon is a dangerous person—"

"My wife has a migraine headache," Mr. Benson told him. "She has not been well since Lane here turned that idiotic party into a circus of horrors. By no means shall you upset my poor wife now. Under no circumstances will you talk to her. Now I would advise you both to leave my property at once." Mr. Benson stepped back and started to close the door.

Marko could not contain himself. "You old fool!" he screamed. "Don't you get it? Corman is a dealer in meth and crack cocaine. He's a criminal! Jasmine is with a dangerous dude. Don't you care that your own daughter is in big trouble, man? What kind of a father are you?"

Mr. Benson seemed about to have an attack. His face twisted in rage. "I am calling the police right now!" he declared.

Jaris grabbed Marko's arm, "Come on, man. We're not getting anywhere." He dragged Marko back to his car.

"That's right, Jaris!" Mr. Benson cried. "Either you get him out of here or the police will."

At the car, Marko was so emotional that he started getting physical. He was ready to go back to the door and make Jasmine's father listen to reason. Jaris had to strong-arm him into the passenger side of the car. Then he grabbed Marko's car keys.

"He doesn't care!" Marko wailed in a kind of dry sob. "The old fool doesn't care about his own daughter."

"No man," Jaris objected, starting the car. "You just got no cred with that dude, that's all. He hardly knows me, and he hates you. He thinks everything we told him was a lie to get Jasmine back with you. He's the kind of a guy who isn't in touch with what's happenin' around here. Guy like Zendon can sweet-talk him and fool him easy."

"What am I gonna do?" Marko groaned, his face in his hands.

"We can't do anything but try to talk some sense into Jasmine," Jaris asserted.

By the time they got to the Spains' driveway, Marko had calmed down enough to take the wheel of his car again. The two boys agreed to try to talk to Jasmine.

When Jaris walked into the house, Grandma Jessie was still there.

"Did the Bensons listen to you guys?" Chelsea asked.

"No," Jaris reported. "We just talked to Mr. Benson, and he hates Marko so much that he's blinded. Jasmine's mom was in bed with some kind of headache. They're strange people."

"Many people in this neighborhood are strange," Grandma Jessie remarked. "I do so wish you lived in a respectable neighborhood with respectable people. That boy, Barko Lane . . . he seems half insane."

"His name is Marko, not Barko," Jaris corrected Grandma.

"Well, he seemed like a madman, whatever his name is," Grandma Jessie insisted. "Is he a close friend of yours, Jaris?"

"No, actually I hate him," Jaris replied.

"And yet he comes here in a dither. And you drop everything to rush off with him on some fool's errand," Grandma Jessie marveled.

Pop stepped in. "Jessie, that's how we are in this neighborhood. We don't like everybody around here. Some of the people are creeps, like this Marko Lane. We been having trouble with him since he was a kid, five years old. But he's a neighbor, you know? He goes to school with our kids. We want to punch him out most of the time."

Pop hoped Grandma Jessie was getting his point. "But when there's real trouble, we help even the creeps. Like this girlfriend of Marko's being with a dangerous drug dealer. We rally round even the creeps, Jessie. That's the way it goes down here. We're like one big messed-up family. We don't get along all the time. But when push comes to shove, you stick with your brothers. You gotta be there for each other."

"I don't understand what you're saying, Lorenzo," Grandma Jessie responded.

Pop let out a big sigh and stared at his mother-in-law. "Well . . . I guess I didn't expect you to," he replied.

After Grandma Jessie left, the Spains sat around their dining room table and had pizza. They'd offered Grandma Jessie some, but she said she never ate junk food. She left quickly and, as usual, in a very foul mood.

"I don't know why she always comes around to stir up trouble," Pop wondered.

"She doesn't come around to stir up trouble," Mom scolded. "She comes to offer what she believes is helpful advice."

"Yeah, right," Pop responded. He looked at Jaris. "So where is this Jasmine chick now?" Then he took a big bite out of his pizza slice.

"I tried her cell phone six times," Jaris replied, "but I'm always blown off to voice mail. Jasmine is so sure that this creep Zendon is going places and she's going with him. She's kinda gullible, like a lot of chicks. Jasmine makes good grades, but when it comes to real life, she's as dumb as a stone. I guess that's why it works out best when the guy is the head of the house." As soon as he made the last statement, Jaris knew that he'd said the wrong thing. Mom was glaring at him. A pizza slice was poised in her hand halfway to her mouth. She had her "mom" stare aimed at him.

"I never knew you had such a low opinion of women, Jaris," Mom snapped. "You sound like a woman hater."

Pop tried not to chuckle as he munched his pizza. His son was on his own.

"Oh no, Mom!" Jaris backpedaled. "I love women, I mean, *not every woman*. I mean, girls like Sereeta, they're wonderful. But sometimes, you know chicks can be stupid when it comes to guys . . ."

Jaris's voice trailed off. Mom's pizza was still halfway to her mouth. She'd not stopped glaring at her son.

"Jaris," Mom commanded, "I want you to reconsider your words and your thinking on this subject."

Mom aimed her pizza wedge at her son. "First of all," she told him, "women—even young women—are not 'chicks.' Second, you must take everyone—man or woman—as they are. They are not one way because they belong to this group. They are not another way because they belong to that group. How're we doing? Are we clear?"

Jaris knew he'd said the wrong thing. He glanced at Pop. Pop looked back, as if to say, "Listen to your mom. She's telling you straight."

Jaris looked back at Mom. "Yes, ma'am," he answered.

Mom finally took a bite of her pizza.

When Jaris went to school the next day, a substitute teacher taught AP American History. They had never had a substitute before. Jaris turned to Sereeta and said, "I bet it has something to do with Shane."

"Yeah," Sereeta replied sadly. "I have this horrible feeling that he was involved somehow in that shooting on Grant."

At lunchtime, when Sereeta was alone with Jaris, he called Ms. McDowell on her cell. "Ms. McDowell, this is Jaris," he told her. "I'm sorry to bother you. But me and Sereeta were worried when you weren't in class"

"That's kind of you to be thinking of me," Ms. McDowell responded. "I have to be here for Shane. Don't let this go any farther than you and Sereeta. But I'm going with him down to the police station. The police need to question him. It has to do with the death of that boy on Grant." Ms. McDowell sounded near tears.

Jaris assured her of secrecy and wished her the best. When he got off the phone, he looked at Sereeta. "Babe, the cops are questioning Shane about the murder on Grant," he told her. "I bet that was him at the wheel the night we almost got hit."

"Jaris," Sereeta cried. "Oh Jaris, it's not fair. She tried so hard!"

"She didn't give me any details, babe. She said to keep quiet about it," Jaris said.

"Anybody but her," Sereeta lamented. "She's the best."

"I know," Jaris agreed, putting his arm around Sereeta's shoulders. "Babe, something going around in my mind. Zendon, he was right there when his cousin was killed.

He's a drug dealer. Do you think he was part of what went down?"

"And now he's probably with Jasmine," Sereeta commented. "They both ditched school today. I didn't see them in any classes."

Jaris and Sereeta never ditched classes. Today, however, they both skipped their last class of the day and hurried toward the Tubman parking lot. They got into Jaris's Honda and took off for the Benson house.

"I think the cops are closing in on the guys who were on Grant that night," Jaris figured. "Maybe Zendon's feeling the heat too." Jaris started the car and pulled out of the lot.

"The Bensons are probably both at work right now," Jaris calculated. "This might be a good time to talk to Jasmine. She might listen to you more than to me, Sereeta. Sometimes a chick can get through to another chick." Sereeta nodded yes.

As they neared the Benson house, Jaris spotted Zendon's van in the driveway. It was the van he used to haul his musical equipment for gigs.

"Hey, he's there!" Jaris noted. "The creep is there. And I don't see either of the Benson cars. So Zendon probably decided to come by and see Jasmine when nobody would be interfering."

Jaris parked, and the pair walked to the door. They passed the van as they did. Sereeta noticed some packed suitcases in the back of the van. "Looks like somebody's going on a trip," she remarked.

The front door stood ajar. Apparently Zendon and Jasmine were running back and forth, packing the van. "Looks like we maybe got here just in time," Jaris commented grimly.

As Jaris and Sereeta walked in, Jasmine was coming down the stairs with an overnight bag. "Heyyy!" she yelled. "Where you guys get off just walkin' in my house like you own the place? I didn't hear no knock and no doorbell ring either."

"The door was open," Jaris explained. "Your parents home, girl?"

"No, and it's none of your business, Jaris Spain," she sneered. "And don't you be looking at me like that."

Jasmine looked guilty. She was obviously nervous, as if she was doing something her parents would never approve of. "Who you think you are, Jaris? You got no say-so over me, you hear what I'm sayin' boy?" she snapped.

"What's hap'nin', girl?" Jaris asked.

"Jaris Spain, you keep your nose out of my business!" Jasmine screamed. "So happens Zendon has a great gig up north. I'm goin' with him like for the weekend. So we gonna be gone a coupla days."

"You're in high school, Jasmine," Sereeta declared. "You shouldn't be going off with a guy you hardly know when your parents aren't even here."

"Oh, they know all about it," Jasmine claimed.

"Jaz," Jaris asked, "is that why you're racing around? You wanna get everything packed and be outta here by the time your parents get home? Girl, you're nothin' but lying, and you know it."

"You get outta my face, Jaris," Jasmine shrieked. "You got no right to stick your nose into my business.

"Okay," Jaris backed off. "Give me your dad's phone number. I'll call him right now and make sure this is okay with him and your mom. Or give me your mom's phone number. I just need to know your parents are happy. They're cool with their little girl going off with some jerk they hardly know, skipping school, and all that good stuff. So let's have their numbers."

"How dare you!" Jasmine screamed. "I'm not your little sister. You can't lord it over me, boy. I'm tellin' you that my parents are happy with what I'm doin'. That's gonna be good enough for you. Now get out of my house!"

"Why don't you call the cops, Jaz?" Jaris dared her. "Tell them you're sneaking off with some shady dude without your parents knowing it. Say some pesky guy and his girlfriend are trying to stop you."

Jasmine glared at Jaris. "What do you want, man?" she demanded. "Why you messing with my life like this?"

"I don't want you getting hurt, girl. It's as simple as that," Jaris replied.

Zendon appeared. He was hefting another big suitcase down the stairs. He had heard the loud voices downstairs. Now he spoke directly to Jaris. "Jaris—I believe that's your name? Get lost, man. Y'hear what I'm sayin'? My chick and I got important business up north, and it's got nothing to do with you. Now get outta our way 'cause we're outta here right now."

Jaris moved in front of the door. "You ain't going nowhere with her, man," Jaris growled in a savage voice. Jaris turned to Sereeta and ordered, "Call nine-one-one, babe. Some sleazy dude is abducting a high school student. Tell 'em that."

Sereeta started dialing her cell phone.

"Okay! Okay!" Zendon responded quickly, putting his hands up as if surrendering. He gave Jasmine a weak smile. "It's okay, babe. I'll be back later. Just chill. This guy's nuts. I think he's gettin' violent. See you later, babe."

Zendon dropped the suitcase he was carrying. He came down the stairs, pushed his way past Jaris, and hurried out the door to his van. He quickly unloaded Jasmine's two suitcases, setting them on the driveway. Then he jumped into the van and took off.

Jasmine picked up a heavy vase full of artificial flowers and flung it at Jaris. It barely missed his head, shattering against the wall behind him.

"I hate you, Jaris Spain," Jasmine sobbed. "I'm eighteen. I can make my own decisions! You've just ruined my whole life." She turned and ran upstairs, sobbing loudly all the way.

Jaris rummaged through a small phone directory and found Mr. Benson's business number. "Mr. Benson?" he asked curtly.

"Yeah, right here," the man replied.

"Get home right now, dude. ASAP," Jaris barked into the phone. "Your daughter was just trying to run off with Zendon Corman. She needs a father right now, man."

"What? Who the heck is this?" Mr. Benson demanded.

"Get home man, I'm not kidding you," Jaris ordered, slamming down the phone.

Jasmine came halfway down the stairs. "You won't get away with this, Jaris," she screamed at him. "You're ruining everything for me. Zendon was going to let me sing at his gig. I'd be singing at a club tonight. You spoiled all that. You ain't getting away with ruining my life. You neither, Sereeta. I blame you just as much."

Jasmine didn't know that Jaris had placed a call to her father and that he would be storming in shortly. She still believed she could frighten Jaris and Sereeta off, call

Zendon on his cell, and get away with him after all.

Jaris and Sereeta kept Jasmine busy by telling her about Zendon. At this point, they didn't care whether she believed them. They just needed to keep her in the house until her father got there.

CHAPTER TEN

When Mr. Benson screeched into the driveway, Jasmine's eyes widened. Mr. Benson ran into the house and fixed his angry eyes on Jaris. "You!" he yelled at Jaris. "What are you going in my house without my permission? You are a trespasser. I shall call the police—"

"Go ask your daughter," Jaris replied. "She and Zendon Corman were going off together, and they said you were fine with that."

"Daddy!" Jasmine sobbed in a faltering voice. "Oh, Daddy! I'm so glad you're home." She rushed into her father's arms. "You don't know what I've been through. Jaris and Sereeta busted in here. Me and

Zendon were just talking, and they like terrorized us, Daddy!"

Mr. Benson had happened to see the suitcases in the driveway. "Sweetheart," he asked, "what are your suitcases doing in the driveway?"

"Oh," she stammered, "I packed them just to see if everything would fit. You know . . . for next year, when I go to college and stuff."

Mr. Benson went outside. Zipping open the suitcases, he found them packed with most of Jasmine's clothing. Then he went upstairs to find her bedroom closet almost empty. The expression on Mr. Benson's face changed to rage.

"You *were* running away with Zendon, weren't you?"

"No, no, Daddy, I swear!" Jasmine gasped. "Jaris is l-lying."

"You were going to ditch school and break our hearts," he accused her. "Break your mother's heart and mine for some thug you just met. How dare you Jasmine? After all your mother and I have done for you. How dare you plan such a cruel betrayal." Mr. Benson's voice was heavy with grief and anger.

"No! No!" Jasmine cried. "It's all a lie!"

Mr. Benson reached out with his hand and slapped Jasmine across the face. She staggered backward and fell onto the living room sofa. Jasmine was sobbing wildly. Her father had just struck her for the first time in her life. Shaken by what he had done, the man sat down and buried his face in his hands. He was crying now too. "Look what I did," he moaned. "Jasmine, Jasmine, Jasmine . . . *why*?"

Jaris looked at Sereeta. They were slowly making their way to the door just as Mrs. Benson was coming home from work. They met in the driveway. Jaris told her briefly what had happened. She rushed inside, closing the door quickly.

Once in the car, Jaris called Marko. "The dude was wanting to take Jaz north to some phony gig, man," he reported. "She had all her bags packed. Sereeta and I stopped them, and we called her father. The Bensons are in there right now with Jasmine."

Marko was silent, probably in a state of shock. "Why didn't you call me and tell me what was goin' down, man," he finally asked. "I woulda come to help."

"Marko, you're a loose cannon," Jaris advised. "We didn't want you around. But everything is cool now."

"How's Jasmine?" Marko asked. "She doin' okay?"

"She's bawling and screaming and carrying on, but she'll be okay," Jaris told him. "She'll bounce back. She always does."

"Thanks, Jaris! Thanks, man! Thank Sereeta too," Marko told him. "I'll never forget this, man. I swear it." Marko was speaking in a sober, serious voice that didn't sound like him.

When Jaris got home after dropping off Sereeta, Chelsea was waiting for him. Mom and Pop were sitting at the dinner table, talking about something that seemed pretty serious.

"Jaris, I got a call from Sharon over on Grant," Chelsea told her brother breathlessly. "You'll never believe what just happened."

"Chili pepper," Jaris declared, "after what I just been through, nothing would surprise me. I'm beat. I just want to take a shower and go to bed. Can your story wait till morning?"

"No!" Chelsea squealed.

"Okay, shoot," Jaris agreed.

"The police went to Zendon's house and picked him up. Sharon saw it all go down," Chelsea announced.

"Oh man!" Jaris groaned. "Mr. Benson must have called the cops and accused Zendon of trying to kidnap Jasmine or something. I don't know if they can make that charge stick, though. Jasmine was really eager to go. 'Sides, she's legally an adult now."

"No!" Chelsea replied impatiently. "The cops came to Zendon's house and put him in handcuffs. It wasn't about Jasmine or anything. It was about the murder of the Lincoln guy."

Mom and Pop then joined the conversation. Mom had talked to Sharon's mother. "Those two boys," Mom explained, "Shane Burgess and Brandon Yates came to Zendon's place to buy crack. Then Buster Bennett came along. He didn't know his cousin was a drug dealer. There was a big fight, and the shooting started."

Pop shook his head sadly. "Looks like Buster was the only innocent one there, and he got iced."

Jaris felt numb. "Do they know who did the shooting?" he asked.

Chelsea piped up. "Sharon heard Zendon yelling at the cops. He said Shane Burgess shot Buster. But Brandon's homies are sayin' Zendon did it. Zendon told Shane and Brandon to keep quiet, or he'd blame them."

"So we got Zendon blaming Shane, and Shane blaming Zendon," Jaris summed things up.

"Yeah," Chelsea responded. "But somebody else saw the whole thing, Jare. Sharon's friend, Keone, saw it from the window of his room. He was too scared to tell anybody. He thought Zendon would get him for ratting him out. But when the cops cuffed Zendon, Keone spilled everything. He said he saw Zendon shoot his cousin 'cause Buster was gonna blow the whole drug business wide open. Buster hated drugs."

Chelsea was excited about her news. "And you know what else, Jaris?" she chirped. "They got some old wells on Grant that've been dry for ages. Keone saw Zendon drop the gun he used into one of the old wells. Sharon told me the cops are there now with searchlights and stuff. They're going down to get the gun. Then they'll have Zendon good."

Jaris sat down heavily. He put his face in his hands for a minute to clear his head. Thoughts swirled in his brain. He was glad at least that Shane Burgess wasn't looking at a murder rap. That was good. Ms. McDowell wouldn't have to help her brother get through a murder trial. Shane and Brandon might go to jail on drug charges, but that was way better than murder.

Then something else came to mind. If he and Sereeta had not gone over to the Benson house, Zendon wouldn't have gone home for the police to arrest him. Right now, he and Jasmine would be out there on the freeway somewhere. The cops might be chasing them. It could have been dangerous and maybe tragic.

A deep sense of satisfaction came over Jaris. He'd saved Jasmine. He saved the little foolish girl. She was a mean, trash-talking little idiot, but she didn't deserve what may have happened to her. Her parents didn't deserve losing their only child in a violent police chase that may have ended in a fiery crash.

"Pop," Jaris asked, "do me a big favor? Call Marko Lane. Tell him what just went down with Zendon. Thanks Pop. I'm tired . . . so tired . . ."

Pop clapped Jaris on the back. "You got it, boy. I'm real proud of you."

Jaris went to bed, but he had one more thing to do. He punched in the numbers on his cell phone.

"Sereeta, baby, just a quick heads-up," he reported wearily. "The cops just arrested Zendon for his cousin's murder."

"Oh my Lord!" Sereeta gasped.

"I'm going to sleep now, babe. See you in the morning. We did good, huh?" Jaris ended groggily.

"Oh Jaris, oh wow, *you* did good!" she told him. "You decided to drive over there and try to save Jasmine. Oh Jaris . . . what if you hadn't?"

"Love you, babe," Jaris murmured before falling into an exhausted sleep.

Jaris got up in the morning, ate a double helping of pancakes and sausage, and headed for school. He was still tired, but he didn't dare miss any more classes.

When Jaris arrived at the Harriet Tubman statue in front of the school, Marko Lane was waiting for him.

"Man," Marko told him in a humbled voice. "I talked to Jasmine's father. He was real polite. He was sorry he didn't believe us when we came to warn him about Zendon. They're taking Jasmine to the doctor today in case that monster slipped her some drugs or something. Mr. Benson told me to thank you for what you did. He said you and your girlfriend maybe saved his kid's life. Mr. Benson said he's sending you a letter thanking you."

"I'm glad everything's okay," Jaris told Marko, starting to turn toward his first class.

"Jaris, man," Marko declared, "you're all right. You're all right, dude."

Jaris smiled at Marko and headed for Ms. McDowell's room. She was there at her desk. Jaris went in the still empty classroom. "I'm sorry about—" he began.

"Thank you, Jaris," the teacher responded. "Shane and his friend are in trouble, but thank God they had no part in the killing. When it happened, the boys ran for their lives and drove off. They should have gone to the police at once and told them what Zendon had done. But he swore he'd blame them and make it stick. Shane has a long road ahead—an uphill climb. But I love him, and I'll be with him all the way. He's my little brother."

Ms. McDowell smiled sadly. "We're all that's left of our poor family."

The teacher started looking over the morning lesson plans. The class wouldn't start for another quarter hour or so, so Jaris walked out into the sunshine. He took a long, deep breath and headed for the vending machine.

Jasmine Benson came to school on Monday. Jaris wasn't sure what her attitude would be. He wondered whether reality had sunk into her brain. Surely she knew that Zendon Corman had killed his cousin to cover up his dealing. That information had to have made some impact. Could it have shocked her back to her senses—if she had any senses left.

But Jaris couldn't be sure. She had to feel humiliated about what had happened at her house. Jaris and Sereeta came in there and treated her like a stupid, wicked child, which was how she was acting. They stopped her from going off with a drug dealer and a murderer. Still, Jasmine had towering pride. Jaris figured the chances were good that Jasmine would never want to see Jaris and Sereeta again.

Jasmine walked alone toward her first class, clutching her binder to her chest. She was usually smiling and laughing and making wisecracks. Now she looked as though she'd swallowed a bag of lemons. She looked grimmer than Jaris had ever seen her.

Sereeta was standing next to Jaris. She leaned over and whispered, "What do we do? Pretend that nothing ever happened? Should we say something or what?"

"I don't know," Jaris responded. "I'm afraid to approach her." He had had all the drama that he needed last week. He had no appetite for standing here on campus while Jasmine yelled at him again.

"Hi, Jasmine," Sereeta greeted Jasmine bravely. "I'm glad to see you. Everything okay?"

Jasmine turned and looked at Sereeta. "Hi, Sereeta," she replied. She looked around to see whether anyone else could overhear her.

"It was just the most horrible week of my life," Jasmine confided. "I don't know what got into me. I must have gone a little crazy or something. I guess that was it. I guess I'm okay now. The doctor said I don't have anything bad in my system. So that's good."

Marko Lane was standing about twenty yards away. He was looking right at Jasmine but not moving any closer. He didn't know what to do or say. He loved the girl. He loved her with as much love as he was capable of, but the whole incident had been painful and terrible. He didn't know whether they could come out the other side as still friends or as more than friends. Marko had forgiven Jasmine in his heart. He loved her too much not to forgive her, no matter what she'd done. He was hooked on the girl in spite of everything.

But Marko could not come any closer to Jasmine.

Jasmine went on to her regular classes, but she didn't participate. She took notes and didn't participate. In one class, Jaris saw her look back very quickly to where Marko was sitting. Then she looked away. Jaris wasn't sure, but he thought tears were in her eyes.

At lunchtime, Marko and Jasmine had had a favorite spot near an ivy-covered wall.

They'd sit on the grass and lean against the wall. Usually, it was just the two of them, but friends would sometimes join them.

Jaris saw Marko buy a sandwich at the machine, and then he made a dessert choice. He bought something—Jaris didn't see what.

Marko looked around. Jasmine was coming from another direction. Her head was down, and she was walking fast, as if she wasn't going to stop at the usual lunch place.

"Jaz," Marko called out in a strange, frightened voice. His tone was unusual for someone who usually sounded so arrogant and cocky.

"Jaz," he said, "I bought an extra cupcake, with lemon filling, the kind you like." In a weird way he sounded like a little boy, a fifth grader making a timid attempt to impress the little girl who sat in the seat ahead of him.

Jasmine stopped. Her eyes sparkled with tears. She walked toward the ivy-covered wall and sat down on the grass with her brown bag. Marko followed her. He sat down too. He placed the extra lemon cupcake atop her sandwich in her brown bag.

They sat there in silence for a few minutes. Then Jaris heard a sob—a wailing, yearning lonely sob. It was quickly stifled against Marko Lane's chest. He was clutching her tightly in his arms. He was teary-eyed too.

Watching the couple, Jaris reckoned it had been a close call for Jasmine. Zendon had evil in him. His business was selling death in the form of drugs. He could kill his own cousin. He might have killed others—maybe even Jasmine.

Shane saw what Zendon could do. But he saw no evil.

Jaris sighed deeply. He had seen the evil in Zendon, and he had to speak up about it.